THE PITAGONS

THE PITAGONS

EPISODE 1: PITAGONS ON THE EARTH

ELIZABETH PALAS

iUniverse, Inc.
Bloomington

The Pitagons
Episode 1: Pitagons on the Earth

iUniverse books may be ordered through booksellers or by contacting:

iUniverse
1663 Liberty Drive
Bloomington, IN 47403
www.iuniverse.com
1-800-Authors (1-800-288-4677)

ISBN: 978-1-4759-2843-3 (sc)
ISBN: 978-1-4759-2844-0 (hc)
ISBN: 978-1-4759-2845-7 (e)

Library of Congress Control Number: 2012908871

Printed in the United States of America

iUniverse rev. date: 06/06/2012

Acknowledgments

The author would like to thank the following people for their collaboration:

Margo Lovelace
Manager

Timea Sivertsen
Book cover designer

Piroska Pap Szarka
Associate

Ivan Nagy
Associate

Contents

Chapter One

➤·┤◆·•·O·•·├◆·┤◄

Secrets of Our Ancestors

We are in the year 2056. The continental parts of our planet have transformed over time, and our ancestors created new, advanced conditions of living for humans through scientific development. All had been living in one huge metropolis. That city provided everything that the people ever needed. Then, five thousand years ago, the series of natural disasters and the attack of inhabitants of alien planets forced the city underwater for a long time. The people eventually escaped from the damaged city to other planets. Altogether, five million people lived through the last big catastrophe. Our ancestors traveled on a long journey until they stumbled upon planets in our solar system that were similar to Earth in ways that ensured the possibility of life for them. They continued their lives on new planets. The planet Kyara was the largest and most heavily populated, with a size fifty times larger than Mother Earth. The people were not able to return to Mother Earth for a long time. It was their scientific research, as well as their experiments, that compelled them to come back.

The Pitagons are the oldest humans, as they discovered the secret to longevity through their experiments, and they tied the success of their discovery to Mother Earth. In order to achieve longevity, there was a need for stem cells of humans from Earth. After completing their experimental studies, they took those steps that led them back to the Mother Earth they had abandoned. They placed 124 pairs of men and women from the natural human race on 124 different spots on Earth, after having assessed the viability of the chosen individuals. By that time, the conditions for life had once again developed on the face of the Earth. Over the course of time, humans repopulated the planet, and then descendants were born in large numbers. Our ancestors regularly observed the history and development of mankind and were continuously present in the life of man on Earth. Most of the human race that reproduced on Earth, however, was not able to initiate communication with them. They constantly experimented with using the stem cells of earthly humans.

They visited the chosen humans at night, in their own homes, and lulled them into hypnosis so they could take their stem cells. Most of the people who were deprived of their stem cells, which were few to begin with, soon passed away from a grave illness. They had tried to improve the lives of earthly humans but that effort usually failed.

They created the first human race that was able to achieve longevity through constantly using stem cells.

In the year 2056, the sole city of our ancestors emerged from the sea as the last refuge of mankind. Lifting the city required knowledge of earthly humans, which in this case was acquired in a very mysterious way. A son of a scientist family, the Simons, living in Miami had conducted numerous experiments with the intent to contact humans living on other planets. His signals were intercepted accidentally by our ancestors. They observed the young man and his family at the time when they received this information and determined that this young scientist would be the one to help during the enormous crisis that would soon threaten Earth. He would be the only one among the earthly humans who could absorb the mighty power and knowledge.

They regularly received the signals sent from the brain-machine, and then, after a thorough analysis and with time of the essence, they quickly decided to send a message to the young man.

Chapter Two

⊱⊱⊶⊙⊷⊰⊰

On the Path to the Secret

I t was summertime in Miami, and even though the hurricane season hadn't begun yet, the air was very humid. The only child of the Simon family was sitting in front of the brain-machine again. This family of four spent a lot of time together. Frank Sr., aged seventy-six and the grandfather, was a tall, lean, athletically built man, fit both physically and mentally. He had been devoted to his wife, Ella, who had passed away last year. Both of them had dedicated their entire lives to the study of mathematics, as well as participating in space research and its development. Over the years, Frank Sr., or "Grandfather Frank," had passed along most of his knowledge to his grandson, twenty-three-year-old Adrian, a tall, handsome, blond-haired young man. Obsessed with scientific work, Adrian was studying math and physics at the university. His parents, Frank Jr. and Emma, had retired from their jobs.

Now, Emma stepped into Adrian's room. "Lunch is ready, honey."

"I'm coming in a second," he answered. He was working on creating a software program, but it just wouldn't work. He made multiple attempts, but something wasn't quite right. He tried it again and again, and then he decided to test how the program functioned. He typed the following on the screen as a trial:

This is Earth. I am Adrian.

There was no answer. He started to lose hope that the completed program would function as he tried it repeatedly without any success.

Finally, there was a sudden green flash, and a map was projected on the screen. A blinking green dot appeared on the map. Adrian called to his family, and they were all captivated by this spectacle. The map wasn't familiar to anyone, so they were not able to determine the exact location of the blinking dot.

"Come have lunch," said Emma, ushering everyone to the table.

"I'm coming in a second," replied Adrian, as the others filed out of his room. He stood up from his desk and headed toward the kitchen. He was already at the kitchen door when he heard the brain-machine beep and make a sharp sound. He turned around, with all of his family right behind him.

"What's making such a noise?" Grandfather Frank asked.

"It's my machine."

Everybody stood in front of the machine, and in that moment, three blinking green dots appeared on the screen.

"What is this supposed to be!" asked Adrian's father.

"Adrian!" Emma exclaimed. "You did it! The program works. You've done a great job, my son. Do you know where the blinking dots are coming from?" She looked curiously at her son.

"I absolutely do not," Adrian admitted. "I just wanted to make contact with aliens; that's it so far. I didn't know whether anyone would answer. Should I continue? I'm thinking I should write something back to them … maybe."

Adrian typed: *We are on Earth.*

The writing instantly disappeared. In a short while, an answer arrived: *We are also on the Earth, with our city deep beneath the ocean. We are victims of natural disaster.*

The screen went blank yet again and Frank Sr. burst out saying, "This is the Bermuda Triangle! Someone is fooling you, my son. You don't have to take it seriously." He waved his hand dismissively.

"It's not a joke, Grandpa!" Adrian insisted. "This is real."

"Why do you say that?"

"Perhaps you just don't want it to be real," Adrian suggested.

The grandfather smiled at his grandson. "All right, let it be real."

"Something will happen—you'll see," Adrian said.

"Son, you know there are miracles, and there always have been. Many, many years ago, it so happened that the continental parts of our planet were reshaped. Earthquakes beneath the seas created tsunamis, and what were once dry lands are now underwater."

"Come on, everybody," Emma interrupted. "Let's have lunch."

The family returned to the kitchen and sat down around the large round table, which was placed in the middle of the kitchen, in chairs that were reminiscent of royal thrones. They ate their meal quietly. Emma, the only female member of the household, circled around the table as she tended to the family. Adrian kept shifting his legs under the table, seeming very agitated. Finally, his father broke the silence.

"A long time ago I heard a true story. I was a young boy then, and I used to go over to our neighbor's," Frank Jr. said, "He was an elderly man, a master tailor, and he used to tell me stories as he was working away. One time, he told me a very interesting story about the Bermuda Triangle. If you want, I'll tell you the story now."

"I can't wait to hear it," said Adrian.

His father wiped his mouth with his napkin and said, "My neighbor, the old tailor, went out to sea because he wanted some rest from his tedious work. He decided to take a fishing trip, so he rented a fine sailboat. In the early morning hours, his boat was gently rocking on the water. With barely a breeze in the air, the boat sailed along very slowly. The tailor dozed off every now and again, and the boat drifted for a good three hours. Just as he was about to fall asleep completely, the tailor felt something softly brush his back. He quickly jumped up and turned around … and saw two strange men towering over him. He quivered and then fell back into his chair, his eyes tightly shut in fright. In a few moments, as he dared to open his eyes again, he found that the men had vanished. He tried to turn the boat around to head home, but a strong wave washed against the side of the boat and then a whirlpool formed in the water around the boat. 'This is the end!' the tailor shouted.

"As the whirlpool gradually became wider and more rapid, the tailor crawled back to his chair and sat down, holding on to it as tightly as he could. 'This is where I'll perish!' he yelled. 'No one knows that I'm here!' By that time, he was surrounded by an enormous wall of water, and his boat twirled around and around as if it was going down into the sea. The old man closed his eyes to avoid watching his fate, but then the spinning of the waves slowly stopped, and he heard the boat grinding and gently beginning to slide, with the hull creaking and rustling, as the boat finally came to a stop. He opened his eyes and found himself in a large chamber. He was still sitting in his chair on his boat, which was now perfectly motionless. He looked up and saw a gap had opened on the chamber's wall, allowing a view into a distance. He sat there, petrified, as a powerful light blinded him briefly. But when he started to regain his vision, he saw in the distance the bustling of a vibrant city, where car-like objects were swimming through the air with people sitting inside of them. And what's more, all of this went on in total silence.

"'It's better if I close my eyes,' the tailor mumbled, 'because it must be a dream anyway. It just can't be real.' He felt the gentle stroke for a second time, but now it was on his shoulder. He opened his eyes, and the two giant men were standing right in front of him again. Both men stood at more than eight feet tall. Right then, the old tailor just fainted and collapsed. When he awoke, his boat was on the surface again, rocking smoothly in calm seas. My dear friend, the old tailor, died several years ago, but whenever the two of us were alone, we always talked about the secret of the Bermuda Triangle."

"Dad, how old were you when the old tailor told you this story?" asked Adrian.

"I was eight years old. I always loved listening to his stories because he truly had some beautiful ones to tell. Every time he told me stories, it just filled my heart with joy. But he never told this particular story to anyone but me. For a long time, I thought he just made it up especially for me. When I visited him at his deathbed, however, he told his old story again. Finally, he said, 'I would like to see them once more, even though I know that it's impossible now.' I held his hand, and he stared at me intensely. Then he whispered this softly: 'Son, look behind you! They are here!' I looked back, and behind me were the two tall men, bowing down on their knees. I stared at them in shock, feeling totally astounded. Then I saw the tears streaming out of the old tailor's eyes as he uttered his last words. He said, 'Do you believe it now, son?' I assured him that I did, but before I could finish speaking, he was gone from this world, and the two strangers had disappeared."

"Dad, is this true?" Adrian asked skeptically.

"You know, many people experience such a thing, but few will ever talk about it," his father answered.

"Is it possible that this strange city is close to us?" Adrian wondered.

"Everything is possible, including the chance that the city really exists, even though none of us humans ever have discovered it."

Grandfather Frank pushed his plate away and gazed forward, seemingly lost in thought. Then he said, "My opinion is that whether there is truth to it or not, we find ourselves talking about strange beings and aliens, and we hear a lot of information about their possible existence. No one comes forward with a statement that aliens truly exist. If the government does know about them, no one would say anything—the government would keep quiet because published reports about such news perhaps would cause trouble. That could lead to panic among people, with peace and security threatened all around the world. It's all politics, you know—really tough politics, but it is necessary."

Grandfather was interrupted suddenly by a news report on

the radio playing in the kitchen. "Unrest erupted in the Italian capital city of Rome today," the announcer said. "Yesterday, terrorists tried to assassinate the Pope, but fortunately, the potential assassin's bullet missed the pontiff. Today, however, thousands stampeded onto the streets of Rome, expressing their anger, and scores of people were crushed in the following chaos. Government security forces confronted the crowds, and a series of shots were reported."

For a few minutes, the radio went silent, except for the static noise of the airwaves. Grandfather Frank and Adrian's parents jumped up nervously from their seats. Adrian was frightened to see his family so tense. Soon after, another announcement came on the radio, and this time it was directed to all people living on Earth.

"Earth is in danger! Massive unknown flying objects have approached our planet," proclaimed the newscaster. "They will soon reach Earth and possibly eclipse the Sun, which will substantially block sunlight to our planet and allow only limited daylight to reach us. Dusk will soon cover everything, and we may possibly encounter complete darkness. It is also expected that weather patterns and the entire global climate may change as well. The full extent of these changes cannot even be forecasted at this time."

The whole family left the table and walked outside onto the spacious patio, which usually was their favorite spot. It was a beautiful summer day; the sky was a radiant, clear blue.

"Grandfather, what is happening now?" Adrian asked.

The old man stared sadly at the ground as his eyes filled with tears, and he could hardly hold them back. "Maybe the report is incorrect, or perhaps it's all a mistake," he said quietly. "This whole thing is just unbelievable. Earth will perish; we will perish. There's nothing we can do. There's no way to escape and nowhere to go."

Emma was gazing at the sky when a small dot caught her attention. "Look over there!" she shouted. She pointed toward the approaching object, which kept getting bigger and bigger. Suddenly, it stopped and hung in the air. Light beams were emitted from it, down toward Earth.

"That's just what my dear wife and I saw twenty-six years ago," Grandfather said softly.

The spot in the sky slowly started to approach again and grow larger, forming into an oval shape. As it continued to approach, the object appeared to stop and start again several times.

The family members could not take their eyes off the sky or the strange light, even as evening came and the day grew dark.

"It's not coming here," Emma insisted.

"It is indeed coming to Earth," said Grandfather, "and soon we will see it move even faster. It might be here in a moment. It's quite close now. Just watch!"

Suddenly, a shining blue oval-shaped object descended into

their backyard as the family looked on in amazement. The shape darkened and then lit up again in a bright yellow burst that illuminated the entire garden. Stepping out from inside the light was a tall and slender young woman with long blonde hair. A dark green cape covered her shoulders. She took two steps forward and then stopped. The oval-shaped light behind her lifted off and headed directly toward the patio. The family just stared at the approaching light, which closed in right above Adrian. It then lifted him up and swallowed him. The bright yellow light beamed down as it floated through the air about six feet above the ground and then turned toward the strange woman standing in the yard. When it reached her, it stopped and brightened again, and the family could see Adrian and the young woman both standing inside the light.

Adrian looked very small next to her, as she was at least eight feet tall. When the woman spoke, her voice sounded agitated. "Come with me to our city!" she said. "It's deep beneath the ocean, inside the Bermuda Triangle. Soon, life on Earth will perish. Come! Help us save the human race."

The oval-shaped light turned from bright yellow to blue again, lifted up in the air, and in a split second, it disappeared from the backyard.

Adrian's parents and grandfather looked at each other in shock as they realized that Adrian had been taken away. Emma collapsed onto the patio table, crying, and Grandfather rushed across the yard, peering intently at the sky.

"Don't cry, my dear!" Frank Jr. said to Emma. "We'll look for him, and we're going to find our son!"

"But how?" Emma sobbed. "We don't even know where she took him."

"We're going to go to the Bermuda Triangle. You heard that young woman asking all of us to come and help. So we're going to go, and we're going to help," insisted Frank. "Emma, darling, we have to help. The survival of mankind is at stake."

The grandfather bowed down on the ground in prayer. A few minutes later, he stood up and headed back to the patio. All of them felt completely devastated as they glanced at the sky once more.

"We're leaving tomorrow!" Grandfather announced. "I'm going to see my old friend Joe. He is a great scientist, and we are going to need his help. As for now, let's just prepare ourselves for tomorrow."

Chapter Three

Adventure on the Ocean

At noon the next day, the family, along with Grandfather's friend Joe, got aboard their boat to embark on the journey out on the ocean. A light breeze blew, and the boat rocked gently as it headed out toward the Bermuda Triangle. The two friends, Frank Sr. and Joe, were in the boat's navigation room. They charted the proper course and then entered the navigational command into the computer. Frank seemed pensive as he asked his friend, "What do you make of the news about the danger threatening our planet? Could it be true, or is it all just fear-mongering?"

Joe took a moment before he answered. When he did, his voice was somber. "I think the reports are true. We are in real trouble, and all of mankind is in grave danger now." Joe looked out to sea, as if he could unravel the mystery just by staring at the ocean. "The Bermuda Triangle holds a great secret. I could tell you a great deal about that, as I've done a lot of reading on this subject and also collected a fair amount of research material. Countless ships and airplanes have gone missing in that area. Fifty-seven years ago, for example, five warplanes vanished during the execution of a routine exercise. No one is exactly sure what caused their disappearance. Another time, five other warplanes took off from their Florida airbase, and none of those planes or any of the crew was ever seen again. The Bermuda Triangle is one of the two places in the world—the other lies off the coast of Japan—that's called the Sea of the Devil. It has a mysterious reputation, and it holds some of the deepest marine trenches in the world."

"How deep?" Frank asked.

"Inside the Bermuda Triangle, the ocean floor is about three miles deep," Joe answered, "and it reaches a depth of nearly five and a half miles near Puerto Rico. Not only that, shoals extend far out around the islands and frequently cause navigational problems for sailors."

"Not to mention the weather," Frank added.

Joe nodded sagely. "Some of the biggest problems are caused by conditions that also fuel devastating hurricanes. The warm current of the Gulf Stream flows along the western stretch of the Triangle. The current is like a river within the ocean. During a storm, waves on the open seas often can swell to thirteen feet, but in the waters along the Gulf Stream, those swells can be three times larger."

Frank's eyes grew wide. "Do you think we'll be safe in this boat?"

Joe waved away Frank's concern. "We'll be fine. It's just good to know there's a scientific explanation for the disappearances," he explained. "One on side of the argument is natural phenomena, human error in navigation, and mechanical problems. On the other side is a sea monster devouring innocent sailors or aliens from outer space abducting people. When it's a choice between science and legend, who can resist the legend of the Bermuda Triangle?"

"That's true," Frank agreed, affirming his good friend's opinion.

"Let me tell you a story that used to fascinate me," continued Joe. "It's about the area of the Atlantic Ocean—near where we are in right now—that forms the Bermuda Triangle. The triangle's points are located on Bermuda, Puerto Rico, and the southeastern coast of Florida. That triangle spans an area of roughly 500,000 square miles and is known by various names— the Devil's Lost Limbo, the Mysterious Twilight, the Magical Zone, or the Devil's Triangle. Up until 1964, people had no knowledge of its existence—that is, no one knew there was anything unusual about the area. But then, several mysterious and unexplained reports surfaced."

"It seems odd," Frank said, "that nothing was ever reported as unusual before the mid-1960s."

"Oh, there were reports as far back as the time of Christopher

Columbus," Joe informed him. "His three ships set sail in these waters, and as soon as they entered the Triangle, all of them lost the ability to navigate effectively. Not only that, but they also observed strange lights in the sky. It appeared as if fireballs were plunging into the sea."

Frank's eyes grew wide. "In all my seventy-six years, I've never heard that story. What other occurrences were there?"

Joe smiled slightly, pleased by his friend's interest. "The first maritime disappearance was reported here in 1872. An English sailor found an abandoned ship, four hundred miles from Bermuda. There was no sign of the crew and no sign of lifeboats on the ship, so it was believed that the ship must have hit a storm, and the sailors managed to escape on the lifeboats. Still, nothing was ever found. It's not just ships that have disappeared in this area; several airplanes have as well."

"Oh?" Frank's eyebrows shot up. "So it's not just being on the sea that's the danger."

Joe shook his head. "Not at all. In 1948, a propeller aircraft vanished into thin air—along with its six-person crew and twenty-five passengers."

Emma had quietly joined the men in the navigation room and was enthralled by Joe's tales. Now, she asked, "What do you think could be behind all of this?"

"Maybe it's a sea monster!" Joe suggested.

"Oh, come on, Joe!" she chided him. "There are no sea monsters here. They don't even exist."

"Actually, they do exist," he insisted, "and we may just run into one soon."

Emma narrowed her eyes and peered at Joe, unable to tell if he was teasing her.

"I don't think we will encounter one over here," Frank assured his daughter-in-law. "Perhaps near the eastern shores of Japan but not here. Such creatures are really part of the legends of Japan, where they are believed to swallow anyone who will cross their paths."

"Swallow them alive?" asked Emma.

"Sometimes alive, but mostly they prefer to crush people before devouring them joyfully," Frank said. "I understand they look similar to humans, but they have wrinkly faces, their body is covered with fur, and their long fingers have long fingernails on them, while their feet have hooves. And they're great swimmers."

Emma shuddered. "I hope there aren't any of them out here. I'm going down to my cabin now—not because I'm scared. I just don't want to meet them."

"I'll go with you," Frank told her. "Frank Jr. must be wondering what we've been doing up here all this time."

They headed below deck, leaving Joe in the navigation room. Frank went to his cabin, and Emma entered the cabin she shared with Frank, Jr. He looked up as she entered and pointed toward the armchair opposite his. "I was just about to come looking for you."

"I've been listening to Joe tell stories about the Bermuda

Triangle," she said, settling into the armchair. Emma began to feel sleepy; her husband did too, and soon, both of them closed their eyes. Emma dozed fitfully, occasionally opening her eyes as an uneasy feeling came over her. As she listened to the sound of Frank's breathing, she peered through a porthole and noticed an odd flash of light outside. A glaring light flashed about three more times. Emma stared as the light grew brighter. Suddenly, it was right outside the glass of the porthole … and then floated through the glass and into the cabin. The light became bright orange and formed into a shape of a snake. It twisted around Frank as he slept. Emma's mouth dropped open in terror. She could only watch as the snake completely wrapped around and squeezed Frank's body. When she finally managed to move toward her husband, the snake turned to her and threw her back into the armchair with force. After this, the snake carefully let go of Frank, and then slithered over to Emma's body. Frank's eyes slowly opened. He looked at his face in the reflection in the porthole and thought he looked thirty years younger. He tried to stand up, but he suddenly noticed how tall he'd grown—he couldn't stand upright in the cabin. Meanwhile, Emma was in total shock. The snake's grip was so powerful that it quickly overwhelmed her. It twisted around her for another few seconds before it slowly let go of her body—and then instantly disappeared through the porthole, back into the sea. Emma regained her consciousness and tried to stand up straight, but she had grown taller as well, and she also looked thirty years younger. Husband and wife stared at each other in astonishment.

"What has just happened?" Emma cried.

"I don't know, but I sure hope it was only a dream."

"How could we have the same dream, Frank?" Emma scoffed. "This really happened."

Frank was staring at her in amazement. "Emma, you are just as beautiful as you were when you were twenty years old … but you're so tall!"

"So are you, Frank. But don't stand—you'll hit your head!" warned his dear partner.

The man embraced his wife as they stooped under the cabin ceiling, gazing at each other in silence.

"Frank," Emma said suddenly. "Where are your clothes? You're not wearing any clothes."

Frank looked at his own body and realized he indeed was standing completely unclad next to his wife. Then he looked at Emma. "Emma, where is your dress?"

"My dress?" Emma repeated and then saw that she also was naked.

"Emma, look at the color of your hair! You were twenty years old the last time you had such gorgeous, long blonde hair."

"Frank, this is the snake's doing. We've been rejuvenated, both of us. Or … do you think we may have traveled back in time? What clothes can we wear? We're too tall to fit any of our clothes, so how are we going to leave the cabin?"

"We can cover ourselves with the sheets from the bed. And I hope we haven't traveled anywhere in time."

They wrapped sheets around their bodies, but then Emma said, "We don't have any shoes that will fit either, Frank. And something is hurting my foot."

Frank stumbled closer to his wife. "Let me take a look at your foot. Lift it up, and hang onto me." Emma held on to her husband's arm as he examined her foot. Then he crawled over to the dresser and found some towels. "I'll wrap your foot with a towel, so you won't feel the pain."

"Thank you for taking care of me, Frank!" said Emma as she tried sitting down in one of the armchairs. "Frank, even these chairs are too small for us. What are we supposed to do?"

"Let's think! Since we grew so much, how are we going to get out of here? What are we going to tell my father and Joe?"

"We won't have to tell them anything," Emma responded. "They will see how we've changed. But I'm sure they'll be surprised."

Frank shook his head. "If the snake visited them, too, then they won't be surprised. One thing is certain, though, we are definitely not our same old selves. I have renewed strength and a new way of thinking—in fact, I feel smarter. My head is much clearer, and I feel much better. I hope you feel the same way, darling."

"Yes, I do, but let's just try to get out of this cabin."

"Duck down, and see if you can get out the door," Frank

said. Emma lowered her head and Frank followed her. "I'm worried about Dad and Joe," Frank said as they cautiously started up the stairs. "I hope they're all right." As they reached the top of the stairs, they heard Joe lecturing to Grandfather Frank out on the deck, and they stopped to listen.

"Levels of the ocean are greatly influenced by changes in weather conditions," Joe was explaining. "Constant rainfall produces surplus water that then causes pressure to increase inside the earth's crust. This may trigger earthquakes and volcanic eruptions along the fault lines. And the result of that could be that harmful gases and debris will contaminate the air, and the risk of tsunamis could increase. Those gigantic waves are formed by underwater earthquakes, and they spread with great speed over distances of thousands of miles. The height of the waves can reach up to a hundred feet, and they often come without warning."

"That's alarming," Frank agreed, "but there isn't really anything we can do about the weather."

"True," Joe agreed, "but there is another source that may trigger tidal waves. Human error and mistakes can sometimes lead to explosions of oil rigs, where a vast amount of oil spews into the sea. Simultaneously, massive amounts of natural gas may leak out, eventually causing large explosions, which then generate tsunamis that unleash flooding onto coastal cities."

"What happens," interrupted Frank, "if the aliens are aware of this?"

"Maybe that is exactly the reason why they reached out to us," Frank Jr. called out to them.

Joe and Grandfather looked to the direction of his voice. They were shocked to see Emma and Frank looking so young—and so tall. They rushed toward them. "What happened?" Joe and Grandfather asked in unison.

Emma and Frank stood up, and the two elderly men stared at them in astonishment.

"Are you all right?" Joe asked.

The couple stood to their full height, towering over the older men.

"We're fine. It all happened in an instant," said Emma.

"Who did this to you?" asked Grandfather.

"It was … an electric snake," said Frank.

"Oh, come on!" said Grandfather. "Be serious."

"It really was a snake that did this to us, Dad," Frank insisted. "How far are we going? When will we arrive at the specified location?"

"Not long," Joe answered. "Are you both healthy? I hope you are all right. Be glad for your youth! I only hope that the snake finds me as well."

"It must not forget about me either!" added Grandfather Frank. "How young we could become!"

"I certainly would let it take the weight of these years off me," Joe said. He studied Frank Jr. and Emma. "Do you feel any pain or dizziness?"

"Where are your clothes?" asked Frank Sr.

Frank Jr. smirked. "Of course our clothes didn't fit us. We had to cover ourselves with these sheets and towels instead. I'm going to sit down now, because it isn't a good idea to have two gigantic people standing on a small boat. We might flip over."

Emma agreed, and the two slowly lowered themselves on to the boat deck.

Eventually, the sky that surrounded them became completely dark. Deep silence overtook the ocean, and only the soft splashing of the water could be heard.

The two elderly men looked silently at the sky—and suddenly saw a flash of light. Instantly, two short persons and two enormously tall men appeared on the boat, right in front of the two old friends. They were so scared that they knelt down before the strange creatures.

"Stand up!" spoke one of the strangers. "We brought some information to you. We are your ancestors. We live on the planet Kyara, and we have come to Earth in order to help you. Living conditions on the planet Kyara are identical to those in our ancient home here on Earth. We are the ones who placed the first human beings on Mother Earth, five thousand years ago. Now, danger is looming. A massive asteroid is approaching Earth. We do not know how close it will get, so it's best that as many people leave this planet as possible. If you earthly humans become extinct, then our own fate will be sealed as well. We depend on using your stem cells in order to live very long lives."

He pushed the two small persons forward. They were quite short and looked very old. "These are humans as they were five thousand years ago! We live 950 years in this form before a transformation takes place, and then our old forms turn into Pitagons. After that, we become guides to the younger persons. Every young person is assigned to a Pitagon." He nodded toward Emma and Frank, who had been watching as well. "Let me introduce you to your guides," he said to the couple. "From this day forward, they will protect you and pass their knowledge on to you. Stand up now!"

Emma and Frank stood up, and the two Pitagons stepped right next to them. The Pitagon standing beside Emma said, "I'm Emma Pitagon, and I'm at your service. I'm more than two thousand years old, and in a sense, I'm your servant."

"What do you mean by that?" asked Emma.

"What I mean to say is that you're younger than I am, and you don't possess the amount of knowledge that I do. You are going to be in great need of me in the future, and I will stand by your side, protecting you and aiding you." The Pitagon's voice was thin and a bit childlike and squeaky. Her eyes were a little bit bigger than those of earthly humans.

Then the Pitagon standing next to Frank spoke up as well. "Frank, from now on, I'm going to be your aide. My purpose is to watch over you and to pass on to you the best part of my knowledge. By the time you turn 950 years old, you'll know almost everything about the universe. You will turn into a Pitagon yourself, continuing your life with even greater knowledge and guiding a younger person. As time goes on, you will start looking more like us, as you become a true Pitagon."

"What about us," Joe asked nervously. "Are we to stay here on the boat?"

"You will stay here only for a short time," answered one of the tall strangers. "Your guides are on their way, too."

"What is your name, stranger?" asked Grandfather Frank as he stared at the giant man.

"My name is Todd. I'm the leader of all Pitagons and humans."

"What do you want from us?" asked Joe.

"We want to become acquainted with every earthly human who possesses great knowledge. The travel spheres will arrive soon, and we will leave for the underwater crystal city, taking Emma and Frank with us."

"So it was you who took my grandson?" asked Grandfather.

"Yes, indeed, we are the ones who took him. He became a chosen person, for he holds abilities that are truly exceptional."

"Will I still recognize my son?" Emma asked anxiously.

"Of course. Didn't Joe and Frank Sr. recognize you right away?"

"Yes, they did, and they are hoping to receive the rejuvenation also."

The stranger nodded his head solemnly. "You all have been

chosen. Not everyone among present-day humans, however, will be transformed. And even though many will be, still many more will die. We will not take crooks and murderers. They are going to burn inside our booster circle."

"Your … what kind of a circle, stranger?" questioned Frank Sr.

"It's the light circle of Earth, which will be cast upon every city, town, and village, wherever people may live. Everyone will be placed inside the outlines of the circle, and then the chosen ones will be lifted up to the spaceship, while the others will be reduced to ashes inside the circle."

"That makes you all murderers!" Joe shouted angrily. "You are destroying the people of Earth!"

"It is not we who kill the people; it's the circle that destroys them," Todd explained, as if his comment made perfect sense. "Those who are not chosen must return to dust here on Earth, as the planet Kyara cannot accept them. They would only perish there amid great anguish. Death on Earth is a mercy for them."

Joe and the members of the Simon family were terrified, and each noticed fear in the others' eyes as they struggled to cope with the shocking revelation. As they stood there, glowing blue travel spheres descended from the sky and hovered right above Emma, Frank, Todd, and the other Pitagons. The spheres lifted them up with ease; then, in a few moments, they were gone.

Chapter Four

Journey to the Crystal City

After the travel spheres vanished into the darkness of the night, Grandpa Frank turned to his friend and yelled, "Joe, did you see that?"

"Yes, I did, and we got left behind," Joe replied bitterly. "What are we supposed to do?"

"Let's go back to the control room," suggested Frank Sr. "We have to determine our exact location."

Joe followed Frank to the navigation room, but when Joe looked up, he saw a sphere of light surrounding Frank's head like a pink haze. "Look at me, Frank!" he yelled.

Frank turned around, and his mouth dropped open in surprise.

"What's that around your head?" Joe asked, pointing nervously.

"Nothing, but what's that thing on yours?" replied Frank, pointing back at Joe. "Are you seeing the same thing as I?"

"You have a transparent pink sphere around your head," Joe said.

"So do you, my friend."

Joe smiled. "I guess we did get a gift from those aliens after all."

"It's not much of a gift, if you ask me," Frank said derisively. "You must be joking."

As the two friends stared at each other, the spheres started spinning around. The effect was dizzying, and Joe and Frank both closed their eyes.

"I can feel that something is about to happen to us," Frank muttered.

"We can't afford to be left out of these miracles, my friend," Joe said bravely. "You know that, right?"

"I know, but I wonder how this is going to end for us."

The translucent spheres kept on spinning around their heads, but each man was able to see only what was happening to the other. Joe lifted his hands, intending to touch the sphere that surrounded his head, but something pulled his hands away.

"I can't touch it," he called to Frank. "Something is not letting me."

"I'll try it, too," said Frank. He attempted to touch his own head, but he only managed raising his hands to about halfway up. "It's not letting me go near my head either."

"We're trapped!" Joe cried out.

Meanwhile, fresh air, full of clean oxygen, started gushing into the spheres.

"I can feel fresh air flowing around my head," Frank said. "Do you feel the same?"

"Yes, I do," Joe answered.

"How is this possible?"

"Only those aliens would know; they did this to us for a reason. But I would really like to know how long they are planning to keep us here—out at sea."

"We have nothing to fear," Frank said. "The boat is safe and strong, so it can easily weather a storm."

"Still, that's the last thing that we need, getting soaked in a storm," grumbled Joe. "But you know, I'm really curious as to what lies down there in the deep. What are they preparing for, and why are they keeping us here?"

"Don't worry; we'll find out soon enough," said Joe.

The two old friends stood close to each other and gazed into the dark distance. Soon, even the light wind died down, and the boat continued to float through the calm waters throughout the eerily quiet night. All the stars were out, shining brightly against the dark sky. The stars somehow seemed closer than usual—so close that it appeared to the men as if they could reach out and touch them.

"I've got the feeling that I could find the way through these stars just by gazing at them," Joe said dreamily, "if only my eyes could see as far as my mind carries me. That wouldn't be bad. I could scour the entire galaxy. I sure hope these aliens consider this wish of mine if they transform me."

"Oh, come on, Joe!" Frank scoffed. "What are you talking about? You know that we humans are not capable of developing vision to such vast distances. And I don't think that you would be given such a gift upon our transformation."

"I believe it's not impossible that the aliens might have such capabilities."

Just then, the boat began to swing, while the sea started swirling around them. As soon as the two men realized this, they tried to hold onto each other. The whirlpool was quickly becoming stronger. The spheres on their heads began to stretch and cover their bodies. Within a short time, the two men found themselves together, enclosed inside one transparent sphere that protected them from the water, just as the boat snapped in half. All of a sudden, a glowing red snake emerged from the water and headed toward the men, but the sphere kept the snake at a distance. It started breathing fire at them, and although that failed to reach them as well, the incredible force of his fire-breath threw the men down deep into the sea. The snake pursued them relentlessly, and it began to wrap itself around them. But once again, the sphere protected them from the snake's powerful squeeze, and they soon slipped out of its grip. The sphere rushed them deeper and deeper, while the water appeared to split apart in its path. They were surrounded by a massive wall of water that swirled swiftly around them. The snake could not keep up with the power of the whirlpool. It soon lost all strength, and they watched as its shape quickly frayed and scattered.

Frank breathed a sigh of relief. "Well, my friend, we got rid of that snake all right, but if they were to transform us now, we would be able to say that we were 'born in the sack' at the age of seventy-six," Frank said jokingly. "For all we know, it might actually happen, even though it's not guaranteed. Yet we still have to accept the fact that we have the same chance for living as for dying."

"We are alive," Joe said calmly, "and we'll continue to stay alive. That's what I believe. Soon, we will find out where this travel sphere is taking us."

The water continued to swoosh out of the sphere's path as it carried them farther down into the sea. The two old men soon became dizzy from the motion and passed out. After about half an hour, they started to regain consciousness, opened their eyes, and noticed that they were descending slower, even as the enormous wall of water still swirled around them.

"I think we're near the bottom of the ocean," Joe said.

All of a sudden, they saw the gate of the city open in front of them. The sphere quickly dropped away before their feet, and all the water started closing around them. And then, in an instant, the gate closed up behind them.

Chapter Five

><+>-O-<+><

The Crystal City

There burst upon their view the liveliness of an active city. It was busy with flying objects, which looked like cars zooming by in the air. Everything around them seemed to shine with a silver-colored splendor—the flowers, the trees, and the houses. Joe and Frank looked around in amazement at this view, and then they caught sight of a glass house. A lot of people were scurrying around inside, each seemingly preoccupied with an important task.

"They don't even notice that we are here," said Joe.

"Perhaps they can't see us."

"They do see us!" Joe insisted. "I can feel it somehow."

"Then let's just hold on and wait for them to come to us," suggested Frank.

They stood in that same spot for a few minutes, admiring the scenery around them.

"Do you think we are still alive?" Frank wondered. "Did we just go to heaven?"

"This is not heaven, Frank. This is the city of our ancestors, if I understood that stranger correctly."

Just as Joe spoke the words, the leader, Todd, and three Pitagons appeared in front of them. "I welcome you to the city of your ancestors," Todd greeted the newcomers.

"Greetings to you too!" Frank said. "We're glad to meet you again, especially on dry land this time. My friend and I are just happy to be alive … at least, we think we're alive."

Upon hearing this, Todd and the Pitagons all smiled, and Todd extended his hand. As Frank shook Todd's hand, he felt a metal device inside the palm of the stranger's hand, so he quickly pulled his hand back. Todd was not surprised by Frank's reaction, and he lifted his arm to demonstrate its power. A bluish-metal instrument gleamed in his hand; he pointed it straight at Frank. The device began buzzing, and then it directed a strong ray of force onto the man. Frank quickly collapsed, and two of the Pitagons had to lift him to his feet.

"We did not expect your arrival so soon," Todd explained. "We weren't the ones who sent the travel sphere. This must be a malfunction in the system that needs to be repaired. Now that you're here, though, we have to find out the cause of your arrival and learn why you didn't get here according to the plan. Follow me!"

With that, two Pitagons marched on either side of the old men, and they started walking off together.

"What kind of torture machine are you carrying in your hand?" asked Frank.

"Every human living in our city has one," Todd told him. "We don't use it for torture, though. We need it for doing our work. It provides essential protection for us outside of the city against attackers."

"What do you mean by that?" questioned Joe.

"We often have to venture outside of this city, and there are several hostile creatures living in the ocean."

"Why aren't the Pitagons there to help you in those situations?" Frank wanted to know. "Why don't they assist you there?"

The Pitagon walking next to Frank answered the question. "We always help, and we're always there where we are needed, but sometimes our help is not enough, and that's when we need a cunning mind and the aid of science."

"You speak in a rather interesting tone, if you don't mind my saying," Frank commented. "I expected you to have an older and deeper sound, yet I hear a tenuous and squeaky voice."

"A squeaky voice?" Todd asked, smiling.

The Pitagons started laughing out loud at Frank's comment. Frank and Joe joined in the laughter, as they could not help thinking how delightfully amusing these Pitagons were. They could not take their eyes of these strange creatures as they walked beside them.

"Don't worry; when you will turn two thousand years old, your voice will become just as squeaky as mine," Todd assured him. "Perhaps you will look tiny and hilarious, but on the inside, you will possess profound worth."

"How do you reproduce?" asked Frank, as if the thought had just occurred to him.

"We are not capable of that," replied Frank Pitagon. "We can only pass on our knowledge, and after two thousand or three thousand years, when our bodies are completely worn out, we simply stop the struggle with life and fall asleep. This is how our service to you ends, and we pass away. We live a very long life, which is plenty enough for us."

Frank nodded as he tried to understand. Then he looked up and saw the others walking much farther down the path. "We've fallen behind the others! Let's hurry to catch up!"

"You don't have to hurry," Frank Pitagon said. "You're not the first one."

"What did you say? I know I'm not first. The others are up ahead."

"You're not the first one," Frank Pitagon repeated.

"What are you talking about? The first one of what?"

"The first one to step through the gate of knowledge."

Frank walked faster, waving at the Pitagon to follow. "Stop joking with me. I studied and worked enough my entire lifetime. I'm too old for that—my brain can't handle much more knowledge."

"Believe me; you're still young. You can handle a lot more. Compared to my age you're just a baby."

"Don't make me laugh!" Frank snorted. "Can't you see that I'm old, and I even walk with a limp?"

"Not for long! And you are still going to be chasing after young ladies."

"Ha-ha, that hasn't happened in a long time!" Frank chuckled.

"You laugh now, but remember what I said."

"Oh, come on. You're not serious about this, are you?"

The Pitagon frowned. "You are starting to annoy me with your attitude. You have to know that I'm serious about this, and you have to accept that it's my duty to be your guide and to assist you. I always tell the truth, and you must always believe me. Just wait, and one day you will come to me, begging me to help you appeal to the Pope."

Before he could stop himself, Frank laughed out loud. "Why would I do that?"

"To ask him to abolish the unjust law that allows a man to marry only once in his lifetime. Think about living almost a thousand years as a young man! Would you really want to spend all those years with one woman? Please—I already know the answer. I've been through this before!"

"You mean to tell me that you've appealed to the Pope?" Frank asked.

"I did indeed—although my appeal was denied, and in the end, the law actually became more severe."

Frank studied the Pitagon as they continued walking. "I have an idea, my Pitagon friend."

"What are you suggesting?"

"After my conversion is complete, we should try to capture the Pope and bring him to this city. He should go through the same transformation as we have. Maybe then he would become more tolerant and make a wiser decision; he surely would ordain a more sensible law. After all, there is only one Pope in the world, ruling from his throne in Rome."

The smile returned to the Pitagon's face. "You are mistaken about that, my friend, but let's discuss that some other time." Without warning, he lifted Frank with a wave of his hand, and they disappeared from the scene.

"Todd! Did you see that?" Joe burst out as he witnessed Frank's disappearance.

"Yes, I did. This is the next step."

"Is this … what will happen to me as well?" Joe asked.

"Not at all! I have a different plan for you. I hope you took a good look at your friend's face. You are not going to see him for a long time."

"Oh, he only wished to get transformed and rejuvenated."

Todd nodded. "That will be completed on him, too."

"Well, I'm really happy for him, then. But what are your plans with me?"

"I have big plans for you. You will become our envoy on a special mission to America. Your task will be to visit the chairman of the National Security Council. Upon completion, we are going to send for you again, as we are in great need of your knowledge."

"But I am no diplomat," Joe protested. "I'm a mathematician and a physicist."

"Do you know how to negotiate?" Todd asked simply.

"I really can't say that I do."

Todd clapped his hand on Joe's back and announced, "Then we are going to have to do something about that now."

"I ... I'd rather just get the rejuvenation," Joe said nervously.

The two Pitagons walking along with them burst out laughing.

"What's so funny?" Joe demanded. "Why are you two laughing? You just have to giggle at me, don't you?"

In unison, the two Pitagons stopped laughing and said at once, "We are simply delighted to listen to your surprising wishes."

"Is that too much to ask for?" Joe said. "What if I really want to be young again? I've been feeling old for too long, and it's not because of my soul but only because of my body; it's a bad system that gets sick too easily."

"Your wish will be granted, but only later," Todd explained. "You cannot negotiate on our behalf if you are in a converted form. Therefore, your transformation will be performed only after you return to us. For now, you will be vested with strength, courage, and more advanced knowledge, which is all that you need at this time." Todd pointed ahead to guide Joe. "We'll head over to the conversion machine, and by the time you emerge from the chamber, the program will have completed all of the changes." He stopped walking abruptly and grabbed Joe's arm. Joe turned to face the leader of the Pitagons, and although Todd's eyes were dark, he said matter-of-factly, "I just have to warn you, though, that if you are deemed unsuitable, your life will come to an end."

"Wh-what did you just say?" Joe asked, his eyes wide.

"You heard him correctly," Joe Pitagon answered. "Your life will be over. The machine will terminate you immediately."

"I suggest you take it seriously," Todd added. "It is the truth."

"Then your machine has a design flaw!" Joe cried. "Why did you add termination to the programming code? It's the wrong thing to do, because every human being is distinctly different, and there's no way to know who might be suitable."

Todd glowered at Joe and said loudly, "It is indeed possible to know!"

"Then if it is possible, tell me whether I'm suitable now!" Joe pleaded.

Todd shrugged his shoulders, as if he couldn't understand Joe's concern. "Let me demonstrate my telepathic ability. Pay attention!" Todd quickly entered Joe's mind, and his thoughts soared through it, taking control of the old scientist's awareness. Joe was terrified, as he caught a glimpse of the future. He saw what would happen to him and to all of mankind. In only a few seconds, he found out something that always had frightened him.

"Get out of my head! I've had enough!" Joe cried out.

But his thoughts started to drift over to Todd's mind, where he could no longer hear any human voices, only a rush of fluttering thoughts. Joe kept begging Todd to make this stop, but Todd was more powerful, and his thoughts continued to stream into Joe's head at an increasingly higher rate. Very soon, Joe could no longer follow the thoughts that were flashing by so rapidly.

"You must learn to be swift!" thundered Todd's voice. "You will use that ability to save lives—lots and lots of lives."

"I'm too old for this!" Joe wailed, still panting after this intense experience.

"Have no fear! I will make you much stronger," Todd assured him. "But first, you must learn to follow the swiftness of thoughts. You haven't yet mastered that skill."

"I know; I understand!"

"Let's practice a bit more. You have to learn to transmit your thoughts, which will serve you well if you encounter trouble in America."

"I thought we already were in America!"

"This is not America!" Todd shouted. "This territory belongs to the Royal Birds, otherwise known as the Eagles! This is where your ancestors originated. Soon, we'll be arriving at the most important place."

They finally started walking again, and Joe looked at Todd with a curious expression. "Just answer me one thing," he said hesitantly. "Why was everything silver when we first entered the city, yet now the grass is green and flowers are full of vivid color? Is this an illusion?"

"It's hardly an illusion," Todd replied. "Allow me to explain. What were you thinking of when you first entered the city?"

Joe scratched his head as he remembered. "I thought of how unreal everything seemed around here. It even crossed my mind that I might be in heaven."

"Heaven!" The Pitagons chuckled among themselves.

"Why are you always *laughing* at me?" Joe asked as he turned toward them, resisting an impulse to stomp his foot.

The two Pitagons continued to chortle at Joe's expense, until Todd finally put them in their place.

"Get to work, and stop distracting Joe from our task!" Todd ordered. Then he turned back to Joe. "The city appeared in silver because it reflected your idea of heaven. But let's meet the residents of this city now."

"All right. I'm going, but I'm still very dizzy," muttered Joe.

Todd called loudly to the Pitagons, "Take him immediately to the conversion machine; otherwise, his heart will stop!"

In a blink of an eye, the Pitagons grabbed Joe, lifted him high, and flew up into the air with him.

"Stop! Why are we flying? What are you doing to me?" Joe hollered.

"This is not a joyride; it's more like a rescue flight!" shouted Todd after Joe.

With that, the two Pitagons whisked Joe away and disappeared. Todd looked up at the sky, shaking his head with disappointment. "This did not go the way I expected it to," he said to no one in particular. "I cannot send him back to America now. I must commend another human for the mission."

Chapter Six

> ⪼ ⭓ ⬦ ⭤ O ⭤ ⬦ ⭓ ⪻

The First Task

"Eagles! Eagles! Come before me!" Todd bellowed. Within moments, a deep roaring could be heard in the distance, and then a group of thirteen spacecraft arrived at an incredible rate of speed. Each of them was shaped like an eagle with large, extended wings. When they all had landed, doors flipped open on each vessel, and a Pitagon hopped out of each spacecraft. The Pitagons moved toward Todd, and as they approached, they all bowed down before him, appropriately greeting the king of the Eagles.

Todd raised his hand, palm forward, starting a yellow light beam that was directed straight at the arriving group. He searched their souls and concluded that none of these Pitagons possessed any negative qualities and, as such, were fit for duty. After this, Todd accepted their greeting by bowing toward the group. Then he addresses them.

"I welcome you all! You were quick to respond to my call, and now I require your expertise and swiftness. Bring to me the young man who recently arrived in our city, as well as my adopted daughter, Lilla! I shall entrust the two of them with carrying out the most important task before us. They must visit the chairman of the American National Security Council to discuss the catastrophe that threatens mankind and the resettlement of Earth's population. I shall order two Pitagons to aid them, with the duty of protecting their lives and to keep them out of harm's way." Todd pointed at the two Pitagons standing directly in front of him. The two immediately sprang into action and left the scene, while Todd carried on with his speech.

"As for the rest of you, it will be essential to remain invisible but to stay close to our representatives. They must never leave your sight, as they are both equally young, and they have gone through the transformation. As a result, their exceptional height stands out too much among the earthly humans, which may possibly steer them into a lot of trouble."

He barely had finished his sentence when the two Pitagons returned with the newly selected envoys. They bowed before the leader and then stood to the side, flanked by their two Pitagon guards.

"We are at your command," said Adrian.

"I know that it's not necessary to repeat myself, as you are aware of your mission," said Todd. "I only wish to add a few important remarks. Once the negotiations are over, you must pick ten elderly men and ten elderly women, mostly from among the very poorest of people. You must make sure that the selected people have not yet heard of the impending catastrophe and that they are compassionate and honest. We will reward these chosen humans with the gift of our longevity, after they are brought aboard the Eagle mother ship. Now be on your way, and may your mission be successfully accomplished! Remember to communicate telepathically with your escorts, because I want to know every detail." After this, Todd bowed to the group and waved his hand at them. He had a twinkle in his eyes as he bid farewell to the team, and then he turned around, jumped, and vanished in a split second.

Adrian stepped forward, with Lilla by his side, and the Pitagons gathered around them in a circle, eagerly awaiting his orders. "We will complete our mission. Everyone, get ready! Lilla and I will travel on the same vessel with our personal guards and without the aid of invisibility. The rest of you must always stay behind us and remain invisible," Adrian commanded. "Eagles! Get aboard, and keep in mind that leaving the city is not an easy task!" Then he requested permission to take off. "Headquarters, come in! Headquarters, come in! I'm requesting permission to open the city's gate. The thirteen Eagles are prepared for takeoff."

The answer was shortly received from headquarters as an automated voice. "Permission authorized," sounded the announcement. "Keep in tight formation, and follow one another closely as you power up to super-speed. The city's gate will open only briefly and during that time, you will be shielded by a wall of water, but as the gate closes in, so will the wall of water. Therefore, you must use the incredible thrust of Flea Jump immediately after takeoff.

"Understood!" answered Adrian.

Each spacecraft took off with great speed and headed toward the gate. They stayed in very tight formation, and soon they saw only the whirling wall of water around them. Adrian never had gone through such an intense experience, and even though he tried to control himself, Lilla could notice the fear in his eyes.

"Do not be afraid," she said calmly. "Everything is going to be just fine. I've gone through this many times. Just try to remember the time when I brought you here! Nothing bad happened then, just as nothing bad will happen this time around."

Adrian forced a smile as he looked over at her. "Yes, you're right. I have nothing to be afraid of. After all, we are chosen humans, traveling in super-advanced spacecraft, while super-beings are protecting us," Adrian replied.

"That's right!" said Adrian Pitagon approvingly.

"Everything will go all right, as long as the navigation goes well and we don't touch the wall of the whirlpool," advised Lilla Pitagon.

"It's looking good!" Adrian said.

The Eagle-craft kept climbing past the towering wall of water on their way up from the depths of the sea.

Adrian issued the final acceleration command. "Activate Flea Jump!"

With one tremendous focus of power, the Eagle-craft leaped straight to the surface of the ocean in one jump. Adrian suddenly saw the sun shining brightly, and its sparkling reflection glistened on the surface. He looked back to see the Eagle-craft flying right behind them, and then he glanced down to the water again. He noticed with relief that the whirlpool was ending, and the wall of water was closing up. But then, giant tidal waves started rushing toward the coast. They swept across the land, where they flooded houses, washed away cars from the road, and wiped out thousands of lives without a trace. Adrian's and Lilla's hearts both jumped, and their eyes filled with tears as they saw the devastation, but they could not look at the tragic event much longer, because their vessel made another Flea Jump in order to shift into super-speed and reach outer space.

They flew in complete silence for hours before they noticed the glimmer of the Eagle mother ship, which was about as large as half of Earth. They were slowly approaching the mother ship, which was stationed out in space, not too far from Earth.

"I just don't understand." Adrian said, looking questioningly at the Pitagons.

"What is it that you don't understand?" replied Adrian Pitagon, who was standing right beside him.

"Well, I just don't get it. Why didn't you find a solution for avoiding human tragedy with each departure from the city? People didn't know about our launch, and it took them by surprise. Thousands of innocent people have perished. This constitutes murder—intentional murder, I might add."

"Yes, you are correct, my friend. We're aware of this as well, but our science on Earth is ancient. It didn't develop after we stopped using the underwater city. Two thousand years ago, we left Earth to live on Kyara, which, as you know, is the safer planet where we live today. It was only after a long time that we heeded our scientific studies and came back to Mother Earth," explained Adrian Pitagon. "We were not able to build a connection with the earthly humans because we'd been separated for too long. We were only using their stem cells to support our extended longevity. We can communicate with very few people, and even then, we must transform them completely, which interferes with their evolution. A converted human can develop far beyond a normal one, living an exceptionally long life, but the individual loses the ability to have children. We constantly struggle to find a solution for this, but we still depend on the masses of earthly humans and their existence, as only they are capable of creating new life.

"You, too, belong to such purpose. We give you our knowledge, we provide you with a decent existence and safety, and in return, you give us the stem cells and new scientific development that differs from our own. Then, many years from now, you will transform again and still continue to develop, and you will be in need of the earthly humans and their stem cells. They bring the development, while we preserve and cultivate it.

"Few will survive the coming catastrophe on Earth, which is the reason why we came back to this planet. We are able to transport five million converted humans, and at the same time we can preserve ten million others that carry the stem cells, those who would not be capable of extended longevity. This latter group will live a normal life, like any average human. They will be brought to the planet Steel, where they will live, work, and reproduce. Then later, when it is possible again, we'll send humans from this colony in order to bring new life back to Earth. We've been doing this process for thousands of years. This is a cycle that will probably never stop, and it's fine the way it is, except earthly humans tend to think otherwise. They believe that they developed from ancient apes."

"Didn't we humans evolve from apes?" Adrian asked.

"No, of course not," Adrian Pitagon laughed. "Doesn't matter how many times we try to debate this subject, we always get the same result." He settled back in his seat and relaxed, with his arms folded behind his head. "I have a story for you," he said. "Listen carefully." When he was sure he had Adrian's attention, Adrian Pitagon began. "It was a long time ago, in the distant past. It's impossible to know exactly when, but certainly it was countless ages ago, at a time when humans lived for many-many years. Our development used to be unrelenting back then; it steadily continued onward, even as we discovered the secret of successful space travel to other planets. In the beginning, only a few people had the opportunity to live life on another planet. We analyzed if they could endure it. We were only humans, yet we were able to accomplish such advanced knowledge. We even reached the planet Kyara, which, despite some differences, was similar to our Mother Earth. In the very beginning, a small vessel was sent from Earth to Kyara. This voyage to outer space—our first attempt—is remembered by traditional human history as occurring five thousand years ago. We set out with one hundred people on board. We arrived safely and found acceptable living conditions on that planet, but we encountered many hardships and many settlers died. Of the initial one hundred people, only twenty-four survived the radical change of environment. Years passed, and the humans started multiplying on the newly discovered planet. They still reported back to Mother Earth about the newfound opportunities. This was our greatest journey within the solar system, and it revealed to us the existence of several habitable planets around the sun. Our scientific knowledge advanced rapidly, but we never forgot where we came from. Then, devastating catastrophes struck the people who remained on Earth. Only five million of them survived, and they all fled onto other planets. The people on Kyara were the ones who began to repopulate Earth and establish new living conditions. As time went on, life expectancy on Kyara increased, even as it became shorter on Earth. Then, however, we lost the ability to reproduce on Kyara, so we focused on greatly extending longevity. We learned that we could accomplish that only by using stem cells. The only resource we could locate was among humans living on our ancestral home, Earth. To this day, the people of the planet Kyara greatly depend on this resource in order to continue living.

"Throughout the ages, science developed separately on Earth, but in the meantime, we guided humans to reach greater achievements. As a series of massive natural disasters devastated human populations on Earth, and their ability to procreate seemed to be in jeopardy. It was up to us to build one last shelter, the vast crystal city that provides for all the needs of humans living within it."

"How did it get to the bottom of the ocean?" Adrian asked.

Adrian Pitagon sighed and slouched a bit in his seat. "Normally, the city would have the capacity to be lifted above sea level. It was only after the last great disaster that it sank deep underwater. Now, it's our task to work on raising the city back up again, as its gate must open up in order to offer shelter for humans. But this presents a huge obstacle for which no practical solution exists just yet, only in theory."

"What would be such a theory?" Adrian asked, looking questioningly at the Pitagon.

Adrian Pitagon tapped his head with his forefinger. "That's

a very tough challenge for us, which is exactly why we must travel to America to negotiate," he answered. "The city has been trapped underwater for so long that the shifting crust of the Earth slowly drifted over it, which is, of course, a natural occurrence. Now, we must move the people away and evacuate the places that would suffer catastrophic impact from the city's rising from the sea. These areas include the entire state of Florida, Mexico, the northern parts of South America, South Africa's northern sections, and the smaller islands in the Caribbean Sea, such as Cuba and the Dominican Republic. We must save all of these people from devastation, but the big question still remains: how will we do that? We can't be sure of which people will be suitable for life on the new planet." He shook his head, seeming almost defeated. "As a matter of fact, very few people will be able to transform and survive. If the transformation fails, the circle will destroy them."

"Circle?" Adrian echoed. "What kind of circle?"

"The circle that we are going to cast down to transport people out, once two of our largest spaceships arrive near the Earth," Adrian Pitagon explained. "Those who are accepted by the circle will transform and may live on planet Kyara. As I said, we can transport about five million people, all of whom will receive the extended longevity, much the way you have. There will be some, though, whom we cannot convert, yet the circle will spare them and transfer them to another system. These people won't receive the gift of an extra-long life, but at least they will live. Their lives can continue on another planet in the same way as they would have on Earth—or similar to that. What's more, raising the Crystal City may save another five million souls, as long as people make it there in time. From there, we can take them to our new planet. Let's just hope that Earth will not be so severely damaged that we become unable to get close to it."

Chapter Seven

Lilla

"How long has Lilla been living on planet Kyara?" Adrian asked. He was fascinated by Adrian Pitagon's tale, but he was more interested in the young woman who was his fellow envoy.

"Why don't you just ask her?" replied Adrian Pitagon with a smirk.

Adrian felt his face blush. At his age, he should have been more comfortable when talking with the opposite sex, but Lilla disarmed him. He looked over his shoulder to where Lilla was seated as she listened to Adrian Pitagon's story. Adrian took a deep breath, exhaled slowly, and then said, "Please, Lilla, would you tell me how long you've lived on Kyara?"

Lilla smiled, somewhat amused by his shyness. "Since the time I was a child," she answered, "which seems so long ago now. If you are interested, I would be glad to tell you how I got to Kyara. We have plenty of time; there's a long journey ahead of us before we reach the Eagle mother ship."

Adrian grinned, more at ease with her now. "I would love to know."

Lilla got up and found a seat close to Adrian. "Let me tell you a secret about my life that only few people know," she began. "I was born in Dallas, Texas, on May 17, 2033, according to the earthly calendar. My parents were hard-working farmers. My father was a decent man who dedicated his life to his family. He built us a beautiful home out of wood that he carved and decorated by himself. My dear mother was a very beautiful, intelligent, and practical woman, who took good care of the house. She kept it clean and neat and planted gorgeous flowers out in the front yard. We had two white horses—one named Sam and the other, Bako. I had only one sibling, my brother who was six years younger. He was six and I was twelve when the event occurred. It was summertime, and the weather was sunny and hot. My parents had to work out in the fields all day long, just to put food on the table. But during that summer, the drought wiped out everything my father had worked for, so we barely had anything to eat. One day, my dad left the house and came home very late at night, empty-handed. He continued to leave the house each day, but nothing went well, and we noticed that he had begun drinking. The last time I ever saw him, he was drunk, and he didn't even come into the house; he just went into the barn, where the horses were. I went to bed that night, but I couldn't go to sleep. At some point in the night I noticed that it was really bright outside. I walked to the window of the upstairs bedroom that I shared with my brother, and I saw that our house was engulfed in flames. I screamed at my brother to wake up, but he only looked confused. By this time, I could hear the fire crackling closer to our room and knew the staircase was on fire. I had to drag him out of the bed and over to the window. We managed to climb out and into the tree that grew next to our window, and that's how we made it to the ground. My brother collapsed and I had to pick him up to carry him farther away from the burning house."

Adrian wondered about Lilla's mother, but he didn't want to interrupt her to ask. Instead, he leaned closer to her, encouraging her to continue her story.

Lilla blinked back the tears that had filled her eyes. She took a deep breath, exhaled loudly, and then, after another moment, said, "I noticed one of our horses, Sam, a good distance away from the house, was stamping and scraping the ground with his hooves. I whistled to him, but he wouldn't come closer, so I kept on running, carrying my brother as far away from the blaze as possible. Then Bako, another of the horses, turned up a little while later, dancing around nervously, keeping his distance, just like Sam did. I tried calling out to them, yelling, 'Come over here!' at the top of my lungs, but they just wouldn't move an inch closer. It took me some time to reach them, so I had to lay my brother down for a minute. He was totally unconscious by then, and I needed to gather all my strength to put him up on Bako's back. He stood steady as I grabbed Sam and jumped on his back. I looked back toward our house as we galloped away, and I saw the entire structure crumble before my eyes. After a while, I stopped the horses so I could rest for a while. I tied the horses to a tree, and I curled up with my brother in the grass. I was going to watch him until he regained consciousness, but when I closed my eyes for just a moment, I fell asleep and didn't awake until morning. I tried to rouse my brother, but he wouldn't answer me anymore; he was no longer alive. I returned home with the horses and my brother's body, but I soon found there was no house to go back to, only ashes and billowing smoke. Suddenly, it hit me that I'd not only lost my brother but my mother and my father too. Both of them had been burned with the house."

"I'm so sorry, Lilla," Adrian said compassionately. "I can't imagine what that must have been like for you. What happened next?"

Lilla closed her eyes as if she was envisioning the scene. "I found a shovel and started to dig my brother's grave. That took me a while to complete. And even though I knew my brother was dead, I kept looking at him to see if he might be still alive. Of course it was no use; he was gone from this world. I buried my brother and then found some stones to place around his grave. After that, I untied the horses, got onto Sam's back, held Bako's bridle, and set off on a journey to leave this place, without knowing where I would go. I traveled farther than I have ever been, until everything was unfamiliar to me. I just kept wandering without a purpose. I felt increasingly dizzy and weak—I occasionally found water for the horses and me to drink, but we didn't eat anything. All I could think was that we had to keep moving. At one point I fell asleep while on Sam's back, but he and Bako kept moving. When I woke up, we were back in front of the ruins of my home. I couldn't understand why the horses had come back here—there was nothing left. I fell to the ground, completely exhausted and confused … and that was my last memory on Earth. Anything that I remember after that happened as strange alien beings brought me onto their spaceship to heal me. I'm trying to forget all the horrible things that happened to me, but I know that it's impossible to erase them completely from my memory." Lilla sighed heavily and swiped at the tears forming in the corners of her eyes.

"Time helps to heal your pain," Adrian offered.

"I agree, and you know I like it here. I'm happy to be able to be here with our ancestors and learn so much from them. They actually taught me to how to live," Lilla said.

"You were lucky that it was not earthly humans who found you that day. We are lucky, too, to have them help us, because what goes on in the world is just tragic. Look at the horrifying skin diseases that spread as a result of human carelessness. Or just look back in history and see what the Third World War has caused. Even to this day, most of Europe is almost entirely uninhabitable, while its wildlife and vegetation is almost completely wiped out."

"That's true!" Lilla agreed. "Everyone knew exactly what devastation occurs in the aftermath of nuclear warfare, yet they went ahead with it, motivated by their lust for power and in pointless revenge. This is the year 2056, and still the horrors of the nuclear bombings of 2017 continue to torment people—at least those who survived."

"Let's not forget the menace of advanced biochemical weapons either," added Adrian Pitagon.

"Was it the Chinese or the Arabs who first implemented such weapons?" Adrian asked.

"The Arabs were the first ones to use those dreadful arms against Europe, to decimate the population, which already was devastated. All these extreme circumstances then led to the spread of human cloning, which did solve the issue of humans born with birth defects, but these humans are not really humans anymore. They might appear perfect, but cloning and genetic engineering doesn't necessarily create better human beings. This technology still has a long way to go before it's declared a success. And the more cloned people there are, the greater the possibility of mankind, as we know it, becoming extinct."

Adrian furrowed his brow, considering Lilla's statement, and then asked, "How is that?"

"Before letting them on to the mother ship, the circle will recognize these people and the system will terminate them. We endlessly monitor and evaluate every movement of the earthly human. We do intervene if we have to, and up until now, not once have they noticed our existence."

"We will be approaching the mother ship shortly, so we have to downgrade our speed," said Lilla Pitagon. The thirteen spacecrafts smoothly glided alongside each other as they waited for permission to dock with the mother ship. "We will land soon," said Lilla Pitagon. "Give out the command, Adrian. I want to see how well you assert yourself as a leader."

"I will immediately issue the order," replied Adrian.

"Try using our new communications system," said Lilla Pitagon. "It is the greatest and fastest in the entire world."

The Pitagons on the vessel steadily watched the two youngsters. They noticed that Lilla and Adrian were increasingly drawing nearer to each other, and every now and then, the Pitagons whispered and giggled.

Adrian couldn't find the new communications system, so he finally said, "I think I need your help—I can't seem to locate this communications system."

"You don't have to look for it, because you already have it on you," Adrian Pitagon said.

"How can that be?" Adrian asked.

"We have it in the palms of our hands," said Adrian Pitagon.

"Is it in my hands, too?" asked Adrian in amazement,

looking at his own hands. He noticed several trails of light, in a full spectrum of colors, gleaming from his palm. Strangely enough, the sight did not frighten him; he thought of this as something natural. For a while, he gazed at the lights streaming from his hand, but when he turned his arm, strong light beams blasted into a glass door in front of him, causing it to explode and then shatter into pieces. He tried to hold his hand down, but he only made it worse.

"All you have to do is turn off your thoughts!" shouted Adrian Pitagon sternly.

"You have to focus your thoughts on something you want to accomplish; this is called the transmission of thoughts. You're supposed to be familiar with telepathic transfer of ideas," Lilla explained to Adrian.

"I'm going to try."

"Force yourself to concentrate your thoughts and then extend your hand forward. That is how you make the streaming of force stop. Always do this when you use the new communication system, as your mind will make it work every time your hand is facing you. You'll even be able to hear your own voice as it reads your mind, but holding it away from you will make it stop and allow it to work in another mode. In that mode, it serves various purposes—most importantly protecting you from attacks. Use it only when your life depends on it and never in other situations. Violation of this rule will result in severe punishment. And remember that you can only shut the device off with your mind, so make sure to focus your thoughts on switching it off."

"How do I turn it on?" questioned Adrian.

"Turning it on to communicate, you mean?" replied Lilla.

"Yes, exactly!" said Adrian.

"What was the first thing you did before the light beams came on?" asked Lilla Pitagon.

"I was thinking about operating the communications system and then I accidently lifted my arm."

"You're making it more complicated than it should be. Try to simplify it, and think only about the task you are trying to accomplish. Then hold the palm of your hand facing your head, and you will see how it works. You have to know that this is all just your own energy."

"I see. I understand!"

Once again, Adrian focused on issuing the command to land the Eagle-craft. He raised his right hand and then turned it toward himself. Just like that, his thought was instantly communicated and heard by everyone.

Chapter Eight

Aboard the Eagle Mother Ship

Adrian used the new communication system to issue instructions to the Eagles. "This is for all the Eagles: turn your vessels right! The mother ship is awaiting our arrival. I want everyone's close attention here. The command must be carried out with absolute precision. After we complete the docking maneuver, turn the vessels back into launch mode."

Soon after Adrian finished speaking, thunderous applause could be heard from all the other Pitagon ships, as a way to congratulate Adrian on the successful completion of his first assignment. The Eagles descended onto the mother ship and completed a smooth landing. Adrian was astonished by the view inside the ship. There were hundreds of levels, with multiple launch pads and docking stations on each level.

"Watch our Pitagon guides," Lilla said to Adrian. "Any second now, they will disappear with a Flea Jump." At the same time that Lilla spoke to him, Adrian heard the following words in his head: "Come with me if you can!" As soon as Lilla finished speaking, the two Pitagons disappeared at once with a Flea Jump.

"They really did vanish," Adrian noted.

"I told you this would happen," Lilla said with a smile. "That's what they always do. They go forth to carry messages, and then they return right back."

"I heard Adrian Pitagon's voice speak in my head," Adrian told her, "telling me to follow him if I could. He must have been joking, though—he knows I'm not capable of that."

"Trust me; I'm still not able to do that either," Lilla said. "Mastering this miraculous skill takes many, many years. We possibly need at least six hundred years."

"How old are we at this stage?" Adrian asked.

"We are the same age; both of us are twenty-three years old right now."

"So my age hasn't yet changed."

"No, it has not. As for me, I've been living among the Pitagons for the past eleven years, and I have learned a lot from them during that time. They're incredibly smart and well-read people. Their eyes can scan through a book very quickly, and then all the information is stored in their heads. Also, it makes them absolutely furious when they stumble upon false works in the scientific literature of earthly humans. They constantly say that untruthful writings hold back the development of science and slow the pace of progress. The leaders of Earth are selfish, and their thirst for power is strong. They drive the weak to a sad fate and deny them the chance for a better life—life on the Earth is quite short compared to ours. They refuse to recognize this fact, and they don't pay attention to it. Instead, they spend their short little life fighting and torturing others, which ends up making their lives even shorter."

"My family talked a lot about these issues, especially my Grandfather," Adrian said. "He was always concerned with improving the lives of humans, until he got absolutely weary of the endless struggle."

Lilla nodded. "I think that we should get to know the commanders of this spaceship."

In that instant, the two Pitagons that had disappeared earlier were standing right next to Lilla and Adrian.

"And where have you two been all this time?" Adrian asked the Pitagons.

"We have informed the king of the Eagles of your arrival. He is new to this ship as well, but wait—he is already approaching with the queen at his side.

"Are they converted humans from your planet?" asked Adrian.

"They were just recently transformed," one of the Pitagons answered. "The new king was converted, in part, from an old king of ours, and now we have a young and strong leader in him. Altogether, three kings rule the entire world, with Solomon holding the greatest power. Jupiter is next in line, and he is followed by Todd. The queen was once a human as well, but she was transformed purely from her own self as a descendant from a very ancient bloodline. Their responsibility is to welcome and transform the new arrivals on this ship. There's no appointed commander on the other ship, but the search is on to find a suitable leader. The supreme commander of our planet is working hard to raise the underwater city from the deep. Surely you have met him."

"Yes, I know him," acknowledged Adrian.

The delegation was approaching, and Adrian watched its members in amazement. He saw tall people dressed in elegant clothes, with dark green capes covering their shoulders. Then he noticed that both the king and the queen looked oddly familiar to him. For a moment, he almost thought they might be his parents.

"Stop imagining things!" said Lilla Pitagon in Adrian's mind.

"Get out of my head! I can think about whatever I want!" Adrian answered in his mind.

"Think of something good then!"

"This is perfectly good enough for me," Adrian responded.

"Are you trying to argue with me now?"

"No, but they really do remind me of my parents, especially the way they looked in family photos from about fifty years ago."

"I don't think that it would be your parents. Anyway, they're too far for us to tell for sure," Lilla Pitagon said telepathically.

Then Lilla's voice whispered through Adrian's thoughts. *"Be cautious, Adrian, because even though Pitagons mean no harm, sometimes they do not speak the truth."*

"I noticed," Adrian responded to Lilla.

"Well, I'm going to leave your mind then, and you can do as you wish!" communicated Lilla Pitagon telepathically. Then she spoke aloud. "The king is here now, so be sure to greet him, although not the way you would do on Earth."

"What do you mean by that?" Adrian asked.

"Do you know the proper way to use your hands for greeting?" Lilla Pitagon asked. "If you don't, then don't even bother because it's very difficult. Just remember that you have to bow before everyone—everyone except the Pitagons, of course. They will bow to you."

"That's great! I already feel like a king!" Adrian joked.

"People here are very well respected and loved by one another," said Adrian Pitagon.

The king stopped in front of the fleet of Eagles, with his queen standing right next to him. Behind them were various women and men, who were followed by their guardian Pitagons. Adrian was the first one to step forward and bow before the king. The king smiled when he saw him, and then bowed to the boy. Then Adrian stepped over to bow to the queen as well, who put her hand onto the boy's head for a few seconds. He felt something go through his whole body and knew that it was a wave of affection. Afterward, he stepped in front of the guardian

Pitagons, who all bowed down before him. Then one of them spoke to greet him. "We're welcoming you on board."

"Thank you for letting me be here!" answered Adrian.

The rest of them went on to extend their warm welcome, until Adrian had walked around in a big circle and ended up, once again, standing before the king. They stood there facing each other, and their eyes met. *This has to be my father*, Adrian thought. *And that woman is surely my dear mother.*

The king was reading all of Adrian's thoughts, and he finally spoke out loud. "It would be a mistake for you to think that we are your parents, despite the fact that we do indeed look similar to them. My name is Jupiter. I'm one of the three kings. Your parents are not on this spaceship. They are still in the transformation process in the underwater city on Earth. You won't see them for another few weeks, but you surely will recognize each other. Our work is important, as human life is short, but knowledge is power, and so our lives will be long. We will discover the secret of immortality. Mankind shall never perish but live forever in this world. Fire will bring no harm; water will bring no harm; nothing in this world will bring any harm to people anymore."

"It is my great pleasure to have met you!" Adrian said, smiling in return.

"Follow us," said the king, "so you may come to know our strategy." The king turned around and started walking, and so did his company of associates, one after the other. He looked back and signaled to Adrian with his eyes. "Come and walk beside me, son! From now on, your place is next to me. You will become my assistant, and we will work together. We need you and your knowledge to drive us forward. Before we begin our task, though, I know that your duty calls you away, as you are still on a mission assigned to you by the king of planet Kyara. I'm sure you know what I'm talking about, as that was the reason why we brought you here in the first place."

"Indeed, I'm very much aware of my assignment," answered Adrian.

"We will plan every detail of the mission to guarantee a flawless operation, because your life could depend on it. Therefore, I'm going to try to convert you back slightly, which will require some of the earlier information and analysis of your body. This process must be carried out with the utmost precision. I only hope that our plan will be successful, and we will not run into any obstacles."

With that, Adrian and Jupiter headed toward the transformation chamber; Lilla and the Pitagons followed them. Jupiter continued his conversation with Adrian as they walked. "We will have to discuss all the tasks, step by step. But I'm sending you on a dangerous journey, so I have to warn you that you must stay cautious of your surroundings at all times." When they arrived at the transformation chamber, Jupiter stepped aside and directed Adrian to lay on one of the beds. "The system will begin with running analytic tests on you," the king said, "and then it will perform the necessary modifications to your body." Lilla stood a bit farther away from them, so the king called out to her. "Go ahead, Lilla—you do the same!"

Adrian was first to lie down on a bed, and the door quickly lowered and closed. A few minutes passed, and when the door reopened and Adrian stepped out of the machine, he looked shorter, which was closer to his normal human height. Lilla's reverse transformation went smoothly as well, and both of them now stood happily before the king.

"Now you are ready to be on your way," Jupiter told them. "The thirteen Eagles are awaiting." He held out two objects that looked like wristwatches. "These are the command devices— one for each of you. They hold the detailed list of tasks. Put them on your wrists, and they will provide you with telepathic instructions of what you need to do. Do not stray from this guidance under any circumstances!"

Adrian and Lilla quickly put on their command devices, which immediately molded onto their arms.

"Everything will be done according to your commands. We are aware of the dangers of this mission," said Adrian.

"Get going!" Jupiter issued the order.

Adrian and Lilla headed together toward the fleet of spacecraft, closely followed by their Pitagons. Adrian Pitagon jumped around behind Adrian.

"What's gotten into you?" Adrian asked, looking back curiously.

"Nothing. I'm just excited about you being like your old self again."

"Really?"

"Yes," Adrian Pitagon assured him. "And in a couple of weeks, we will come back here again because you will need to go through yet another transformation."

"All right, but please stop jumping around right now, and stay behind me, because the king is still watching us."

Adrian Pitagon laughed merrily and continued to jump. "The king knows that I act like this every time I'm cheerful," he said. "He would actually think that something is wrong if I weren't jumping for joy."

"Just stay behind me, all right?"

With that, the Pitagon finally stepped in line behind Adrian and followed him without all the silly skipping and hopping.

Chapter Nine

⊱ ⟡ ⊰

The Chance Meeting

Soon, everyone got aboard his or her own spacecraft, and the fleet of thirteen Eagles took off to return to Earth again. At that time, none of them realized how much trouble they would encounter on Earth. Nobody noticed the small mistake that was made during transformation.

The Eagles followed each other, flying in very tight formation as they lifted into space. They all lined up behind the Eagle mother ship and flew out of sight with great speed. Lilla calmly observed the event on her own screen, thinking that this was probably the way it should be.

The Eagles take care of us, so nobody needs to know this, she thought.

But then Adrian Pitagon spoke in her mind. *"Little girl, your soul is so pure! Can you think of nothing else but pleasant thoughts?"*

"Why? Am I wrong for thinking this way?" she responded telepathically.

"No, but you will have to learn to fight. Or have you already forgotten that earthly humans are not gentle aliens from outer space?"

And then Lilla Pitagon said aloud, "They will look at you and capture you right away."

Lilla's eyes widened. "Capture me—like, taking me as a prisoner?"

"Precisely, yes!" said Lilla Pitagon.

"You can't be serious … are you?"

Lilla Pitagon nodded somberly. "I am sensing trouble."

"What kind of trouble?"

"It will soon become clear, but I think that performing the reverse transformation may have been … a mistake."

"A mistake?" Lilla asked. "But why?"

Lilla Pitagon squirmed uncomfortably, and when she responded, her voice sounded unsettled. "I believe that once we reach Earth, you and Adrian will grow very tall again. And by then, it will be too late to abort the mission, and you will have to carry on, regardless of your appearance. However, this will complicate the matter, as if this weren't already the biggest trouble that Earth has ever had."

Lilla looked quickly from Lilla Pitagon to Adrian, her eyes wide. "Should we believe her, Adrian? Do you think she's telling the truth?"

Adrian shrugged easily. "Let's hope not."

"But it's true! It's true!" the two Pitagons said together with their squeaky voices.

"Quiet, both of you!" Adrian commanded.

"No, we are not going to be quiet!" they replied at once, and then they burst into a fit, jumping, flipping, tousling their hair, and pressing their cheeks with their hands as they puckered their lips, blowing air toward Adrian and Lilla.

The two youngsters looked at the command devices on their arms and quickly flicked through the list of instructions, which were popping up with blazing speed before their eyes, but then they just shook their heads.

"I'm not finding any evidence of possible problems or dangers, as our Pitagons suggested," Adrian said confidently.

"I don't think that we should rule out unexpected problems," Lilla said cautiously, "but let's not forget that Pitagons like to put us to the test. It just shows that they do care about our success; otherwise, they are really friendly and dependable."

"I agree with you, but I hope we are correct about this. But if they aren't just testing us, then we are heading down a pretty rough road."

"We are not tricking you!" the Pitagons insisted.

"Can we really believe you about this?" Adrian asked, narrowing his eyes as he looked back at them.

"Believe us! We are being good now," said the Pitagons in unison.

"We just offer help in times of trouble," Lilla Pitagon added.

"And if you're ever in need of this kind of help, then call out for us," Adrian Pitagon said.

The Eagles were approaching their target. Some of them revealed themselves occasionally, but most of them flew undetected toward the designated destination—Earth.

All of a sudden, the defense systems of Earth started firing at the approaching Eagle-craft.

"How is this possible?" Adrian shouted.

"They've detected us!" Adrian Pitagon answered. "We have to be nimble now, or they will definitely shoot us down."

"All ships activate Flea Jump!" Adrian yelled.

With one sudden leap, the Eagles crossed the energy field surrounding the planet. And after they entered into the Earth's atmosphere, all of them turned on stealth mode to become invisible.

"We will be landing on the planned clearing in a couple of seconds. All of you remember to stay invisible!" Lilla ordered.

The two Pitagon guides observed every movement of the two youngsters. They noticed that the bodies of the young humans slowly began changing form, as had been predicted, but they decided not to say a word about it yet. Then, in the matter of a few seconds, something totally unexpected happened. The two young people changed back to their original forms—Lilla became a twelve-year-old little girl, and Adrian became a tall twenty-three-year-old.

"This can't be true!" Adrian cried out. "Lilla, you're just a little girl now!"

Lilla looked at her own body. "That may be so, but I'm a little girl with great knowledge."

Adrian studied her for a moment and then asked, "How do you know you've retained all of your knowledge?"

Lilla shrugged. "I just know. I remember everything that I was taught, including the security codes of the spaceship. Tell me, Adrian, do you recall everything easily, or are there certain things you have a hard time remembering?"

Adrian closed his eyes for a moment as he tested himself. When his eyes opened, he spoke confidently. "I remember all the information that I received, too, except for one thing. I can't recall my grandfather's face at all. I don't think that I would be able to recognize him, even if he were to walk up to me." Adrian sighed. "I just hope that he will at least recognize me."

"I'm sure that he will—you haven't changed at all. You look just the way you did before," Lilla replied.

"You really haven't changed a bit, Adrian," mumbled Adrian Pitagon, who now stood next to the young man. Moments earlier, he had disappeared, and Adrian jumped at the sound of his voice.

"Where were you?" questioned Adrian.

"We went to seek help in the underwater city. That's where your initial transformation was performed, so we had to look at the light-absorption unit of the conversion processor. We found nothing of significance—only a minor glitch."

Adrian nodded as if the Pitagon's words made perfect sense. Then he tilted his head toward Lilla. "What's going on with her?"

"She's a cute little girl," Adrian Pitagon answered.

"This is not the time to joke around," Adrian said sternly. "We all know that we're facing a big problem here."

"It isn't as big a problem as you think," Adrian Pitagon assured him.

Adrian pursed his lips and glared at the Pitagon. "It actually *is* a very big problem for me and for Lilla as well. How am I supposed to bring a child to the negotiating table at the American National Security Council?"

Adrian Pitagon waved away his concern. "Don't worry; she will turn into an adult once again as the process runs its course. You didn't experience anything special, so the light-absorption converter unit must have just worked backward as well."

"I'm only hoping that I'm not going to transform again because of some malfunction in the light-absorption unit," said Adrian with a sigh.

"Don't bet your life on it!" warned Lilla Pitagon.

"Why do you say that?" Adrian asked.

"Because the process was not fully completed in your case either. The light-absorption unit went haywire, and it has gone backward and forward as well."

"Do you always have to talk gibberish just to confuse me?" Adrian snapped. "I'm issuing the order to head back to the underwater city immediately!"

"We can't go back," his Pitagon said. "Our ships will not be able to enter the city."

"Why?"

"It's impossible to get in right now," said Lilla Pitagon firmly. "The process to raise the city from the deep is already underway. We must follow Jupiter's orders and simply carry out the task that we were given."

"Lilla will once again return to a full-grown form with the help of an electric snake, so we must wait for its assistance," said Adrian Pitagon.

Lilla gasped and took a step away from the Pitagons. "There is no way that I'm going to let an electric snake wrap around me!" she cried.

"The snake will not ask you for your permission," her Pitagon said calmly. "It will simply wrap around your body."

"Why does it have to be a snake?" Lilla whimpered. "Can't they have someone else do the job?"

"Well, little girl, you should know that we don't pick and choose."

"I'm not a little girl!" Lilla said peevishly. "I'm twenty-three years old!" She glared at the two Pitagons.

"Well, right now, you are a twenty-three-year-old who looks like a twelve-year-old girl."

Lilla sighed, already exhausted from the argument. "All right. Let that snake wrap itself around my body and get this over with."

"That's what we want to hear!" said the Pitagons in unison.

With that, Adrian issued the command. "Eagles, vanish immediately!"

All of them instantly disappeared from the field, as the ships turned on their invisibility mode. Adrian's eyes were scanning the area when he noticed people approaching the spot where the thirteen Eagles were positioned.

"These people must be homeless or vagrants," commented Adrian Pitagon. "It would be better if they don't notice the Eagles. That could easily lead to trouble. People don't know about our existence, so panic might break out if they find out about us. If they carry weapons, they could damage the exterior of our ships. The Eagle-craft can be easily detected, even if one of them just bumps into the invisible vessel."

"I pray that they don't walk in our direction," Adrian said.

"Do you think they would be able to penetrate the ship's walls?" Lilla wondered.

"Oh, little girl, they wouldn't stand a chance!" answered Lilla Pitagon. "They would not be able to walk across the vessels because they are physically still there. The Eagle-craft can sense human energy, as it uses that as a driving force. Therefore, it also recognizes the energy of an earthly human, and the spacecraft will start booting up. The more human energy it picks up, the more visible it becomes. Humans on Earth generally are frightened by this, but there is no way to tell exactly how they might react. I think we should stay alert and try to remain in stealth mode. This is our best chance to avoid trouble."

"So there might be a problem if they accidentally bump into us," Lilla said.

"Yes, that would be plenty enough to blow our cover."

"Well-built men are coming straight toward the ship! There is no way we're going to remain in stealth mode, and it's already too late to take off!" Adrian cried. "We noticed them too late!"

Suddenly, one of the men started running, and then the rest of them followed.

"All right, Eagles, I'm ordering everyone to immediately take off with a Flea Jump," instructed Adrian.

"That's impossible!" the Pitagons called out.

"No, it's not! Do it now! Jump!"

With that, the ships became visible to the man running down the field, and he saw them lift off and disappear in a blink of an eye.

The man collapsed to the ground in total shock. He put his hands together in a prayer as he gazed up to the sky. "Oh Lord, my heavenly Father, please don't take my sanity away. I know that I drank more than I should have yesterday, but make sure that this was just my eyes playing tricks on me, or please let me believe that I'm still drunk and I haven't even seen anything," the man prayed desperately.

The rest of the men who were also running soon reached

him and had to jump over his body to avoid stepping on their friend before stopping to see what happened.

"What happened, Borzas?" one asked.

"I ... saw something. But whatever it was must have been just my imagination. I'm probably still drunk."

"We saw something, too!" another said.

"Then you all must still be drunk, just like me."

"We haven't even had a sip today," one of his friends protested.

"Well, then ... I guess I've seen something like an eagle ... or eagles ... or more like a whole flock of eagles."

"We saw eagles too, but they were much bigger than normal." said one man.

"These eagles were made of iron," added another. "Or maybe steel."

At that moment, Adrian's and Lilla's Pitagons jumped from the ship down to the ground, straight in front of the group of runners. Adrian noticed this, and he telepathically spoke to the Pitagons. "What are you doing?" he asked. In a few seconds, he received the following answer:

"We're going to teach something to these earthlings."

The group of men looked petrified when the Pitagons appeared in front of them.

"Do you see this, Borzas?" one whispered.

The man called Borzas nodded. "I guess I am still drunk after all." He stood up and reached out toward the Pitagons, but they lifted into the air and hovered over the men, just out of reach, and they giggled in their thin, high-pitched voices.

"What are they?" Borzas wondered aloud.

"We're humans, like you," Adrian Pitagon replied.

"Borzas, do something!" one of his friends urged.

"I'll catch them," answered Borzas. With that, he started jumping up toward the two Pitagons, but they levitated effortlessly in the air above the group, and Borzas was not able to reach them.

"Where did you midgets come from?" grumbled Borzas as he kept jumping up at them.

"We came from another planet."

Borzas stopped jumping and stared at the Pitagons floating over his head. "You came from outer space? Who are you?"

"Yes, indeed," Lilla Pitagon replied. "We're the most ancient humans in the world."

"How is that possible?" Borzas demanded to know. "I believe that you are very old, but you don't look human, with your gray faces, big ears, and large, bulging, ugly eyeballs." He stamped his foot in frustration. "Come down here. This is starting to make me dizzy. Let's have a conversation the way normal people would!"

The two Pitagons chuckled at his comment but then agreed. "All right, we will come down to you now, and we will have a talk like normal human beings." They slowly descended in front of the group of men, and that was when they noticed that the group of men was larger than they'd thought. Their eyes quickly counted the members of the group; there were exactly seven men standing in front of them, and the men formed a circle around the two Pitagons.

"Let's grab them now!" yelled Borzas.

At that moment, the little Pitagons turned the palms of their hands toward the men and used radiating energy to stop their attack. The men felt they couldn't move; they just stared at the Pitagons as the rays of energy pushed them farther and farther back.

"What is this? What's going on?" asked Borzas.

"It is gravity control," answered Lilla Pitagon. "And you unruly rascals had better behave!"

"We'll behave," Borzas promised. "Just let us loose already."

"Give us a break, Grandpa!" one of the other men cried. "We didn't do anything."

"That's exactly what the problem is," said Adrian Pitagon. "None of you ever do anything."

The Pitagons looked into the minds of these men and saw all of their troubles and misfortunes throughout their lifetime.

"Should we take them away with us to be transformed into good persons?" Lilla Pitagon asked Adrian Pitagon.

"What do you want with us?" Borzas asked nervously.

"You'll see, Borzas," Lilla Pitagon said. "Your life will soon turn around for the better!"

"But first, you will have to obey me immediately," Adrian Pitagon ordered.

The Pitagons forced Borzas and the other men to kneel on the ground; the men had no choice but to surrender to the power of the energy.

"From this day forward," Adrian Pitagon intoned, "you earthly humans will listen to our words, take our knowledge, and accept our graciousness into your lives."

"We'll accept anything! Just please let us loose!" one man pleaded.

"There will be no violence! There will be no inhumanity of any kind! Every person has a right to live in this world and to live without violence. And remember this well: you will never hurt another human being again! No one is superior because of his strength; everyone is equal. Do you all understand?"

"No!" yelled Borzas defiantly. "I'm the boss here!"

"Yeah, he really is the boss," acknowledged all the other men in unison.

"In that case, we'll have to teach you all a lesson," said Adrian Pitagon. "We're taking you all to the conversion chamber, because every time I take my eyes off of you, you start acting up again."

"Listen, Grandpa, you can't be serious!" Borzas snorted. "We're not coming with you. We aren't leaving Earth."

"Stop arguing!" Adrian Pitagon commanded. With that,

both Pitagons focused their energy on the group to force them to be obedient.

"What kind of power do you have within you?" wondered Borzas.

"This is knowledge, and knowledge is power," Lilla Pitagon.

"Stand up, Borzas!" Adrian Pitagon commanded.

Borzas jumped up right away, and his eyes became locked in a hypnotic stare with the Pitagons. They could tell by the look on his face that he was slowly becoming obedient, and they were pleased with their ability to change such a strong and violent man into a peaceful person. At that moment, however, two Eagle spaceships appeared overhead and descended on the field, which prompted the men to quickly throw themselves on the ground for cover. The next time the men looked up, the Pitagons had vanished from sight completely, and the Eagle spaceships lifted into the air, disappearing swiftly into the darkness of the night sky. The men on the ground were not sure what had happened, and they kept lying in the grass until they gradually realized that the strange beings were gone, and they no longer felt the powerful grip of their energy. After that, they all got to their feet to look up to the sky, but they saw nothing. They took off running in all directions until they scattered from the scene.

Adrian confronted the arriving Pitagons. "What was the purpose of that?"

"We put those earthly humans to the test and found that two of them have character that is suitable for development. These two humans should come with us, but the others are too unintelligent to be transformed. Those men will soon be among the first to enter the circle, and when they do, that day will be their last," explained Adrian Pitagon.

"Fine, bring on board the individual named Borzas and the other who is worthy. Take them to our house in Miami while I'm negotiating on the Eagle mother ship. They still have to pass the trials, just like everybody else," said Adrian.

Chapter Ten

><

The Ruby Crystal

The door of the great conference hall opened, and a four-thousand-year-old Pitagon named David entered. In his hand he held a ruby-colored crystal matrix. Its bright glow lit the entire chamber. "I'm here looking for the chosen earthly human called Adrian," he said.

Another Pitagon stepped forward to bow before the Pitagon, saying, "You will find the chosen one named Adrian on board his spaceship. I suggest you call upon him telepathically and summon him to this great chamber. It's time for him to meet those he'll be working with in the future."

"I will do as you say," answered the old Pitagon.

Soon, Adrian and Lilla, along with their Pitagon guides, appeared in the great hall. Every Pitagon and transformed human turned and bowed to them in greeting.

The elderly Pitagon stepped out of the crowd to face them.

"Adrian! This crystal matrix belongs to you now," he said. "I'm handing it over to you with a warning about its special nature. As long as you keep it in your possession, it will keep you from getting into trouble. But if you lose it, your knowledge will decline, and you will experience a rapid aging process, which eventually will end with your natural human death. A new chosen human will then take your place. For these reasons, I offer you this warning to always keep this crystal matrix in such a place that another earthly human may not take hold of it. If you lose it for whatever reason, you will pay for it with your life. This crystal holds the key to living longer than any human ever could. If someone seeks your life, however, that person could succeed by taking this from you, and you won't be able to stop him. The power of the matrix will transfer to the one who is holding it."

"What should I make of this strange theory?" asked Adrian.

"In your current form, as you pass the age of one thousand, you will turn into a Pitagon. This crystal will aid you through this transition, and with the help of its power, you may continue to live young forever—essentially, becoming immortal. The crystal also will assist you in finding a way for humans to live underwater after living on land becomes impossible. Always keep this crystal with you!" the old Pitagon said. He stood erect, holding the crystal outward in his hand. "Now I, David, the four-thousand-year-old Pitagon, will hand the crystal matrix over to you. Extend your right hand to me with an open palm and receive my powers, as I shall die."

Adrian took the crystal, held it in his open hand, and watched as the enormous power weaved around him with a glowing red stream of light. After a moment, the light subsided and returned to the palm of his hand. Then the crystal matrix completely blended into his hand and vanished from view inside his palm.

David's body scattered into ashes before everyone's eyes. A light breeze picked up the ashes, carrying them out the door, through the side gate, and out into the vast universe to be gone forever.

Adrian Pitagon stepped forward to address the people in the great hall. "We must communicate an important message to the humans on Earth. Their planet has come under a serious threat. This time, it is not due to the fault of mankind but the result of constant motion of the galaxies. As many different gravitational forces cause collisions and fractures of matter, they produce debris of various sizes. Some are smaller asteroids and some are larger, all of which end up traveling in space at great speed and eventually hitting planets such as Earth." He looked out over the assembled crowd and saw everyone looking at him intently. He raised his voice and continued. "Multiple asteroids are on collision course with Earth at this moment. According to our calculations, they will reach the planet within eight to fifteen months. Rescuing the human race is our top priority, and we must relocate as many people as possible to the planets Kyara and Steel." He turned to the chosen young man. "Adrian! The responsibility rests on your shoulders to bring the news to the leaders of your world. You have the best of our Pitagons at your side—thirteen highly trained guides, who will assist you every step of the way."

"You are missing one thing, my friend," Adrian said. "Lilla's conversion must be corrected, because I'm not leaving without her."

"Indeed, you are right!" Lilla Pitagon said. "King Jupiter did entrust both of you with carrying out this mission. I'm going to see to it that the two of you will be able to go together."

"Does this mean that the snake will wrap around me now?" Lilla asked in a shy and frightened voice.

"Sweetheart, you already promised us that this wasn't going to be a problem for you," whispered the Pitagon standing beside the girl.

"That was then. Now, I don't want it anymore! I'd rather have you put me into the conversion chamber!"

"I can't do that. Its program obviously contains a flaw in connection with your data set. Only the electric snake is able to resolve your problem. Please let us go forward with this, because you cannot help your friend in your current form."

"All right," Lilla sighed. "I understand. Let the snake do its job!"

The electric snake slithered forth and gently twisted itself around the girl; then it starting to spin around her body. The motion seemed to be aglow with a bright orange light, which completely covered up the outlines of the girl. The snake spun ever faster, until it levitated in the air and rotated around very swiftly. Then, in a split second, it simply became still, and everyone saw Lilla standing in the center as a transformed young woman again. Its duty fulfilled, the snake disappeared from the scene. The crowd of onlookers in the great hall greeted the girl with a loud round of applause. She now stood before them as a gorgeous woman. Lilla quickly stepped over to Adrian, who happily embraced his dearest friend. They walked out together toward the launch pads, where the thirteen Pitagons were awaiting them by each of their Eagle ships. Everyone took their places, and then the Eagles lifted off, one by one, toward the target of their grand assignment, Mother Earth.

From that day on, all spaceships began broadcasting instructive presentations about the ancient times. Some were about the history of the world, the wars people had fought, and accomplishments they had achieved, while others discussed the destructive forces of nature and the impact on civilization.

"Forces of nature," the presentations proclaimed, "are the mightiest powers known to man and have been a source of admiration as far back as the dawn of civilization. People have been trying to harness the power for ages, but they always lacked the knowledge and technology to effectively put such great forces to work. It's unthinkable to even attempt to influence these awesome raw forces, let alone try to contain them or to stop the occasional devastation they cause to the environment. Man has no choice but to learn to accept them and coexist with them. Over the course of history, humans started using the energy of the wind, the healing power of hot springs and medicinal herbs, and the energy of the sun as a source of heat and light. No one can stop the wheel of history from turning, but humanity's fate and progress lies within our own hands. If we join together, our power will be strong enough to work wonders. A civilized human being creates, builds, and produces great works, but not everyone is capable of this. Other savage humans only express themselves through violent means, which occasionally stifles the wonderful human desire to create."

In the meantime, the two old friends, Frank Sr. and Joe, did undergo the transformation into a youthful form, which they previously had anticipated. By this time, they were working in the main control room of the underwater city alongside hundreds of others. Their efforts finally seemed to be paying off, as they were nearing completion of the task with which King Jupiter had entrusted them. Only the chosen humans and their Pitagons were allowed to work on finding the solution. The mission was focused on the reconstruction effort of the city's lifting mechanism, which required the restoration of an ancient energy grid. Ancestors had used clean energy and had positioned energy link points in one thousand separate places, which created a network that spanned the entire globe. This grid supplied the necessary clean energy to the light-absorption control system of the city's lifting mechanism, which would ensure that the process to raise the city would get underway successfully. They knew that they had no time to waste, as this city was to become the last refuge on Earth for humans.

Frank Pitagon stood close enough to listen in on the conversation of the two friends, and finally, he felt that he had to speak. "We don't have to look for the link points; they will link up automatically, once the city emerges onto the surface, and then it will be ready to receive the flow of clean energy. First, we have to fix the energy regulator, which supplies power to the main control system. If we are able to repair that, then the process will kick in, and the city will rise from the deep. The second challenge we face is the damage to the city's protective shield, which would block the flow of energy if we leave it in its current shape. Our plan has a chance to work flawlessly only after a successful restoration of the shield."

"Thank you for sharing this information with us," Joe Pitagon replied. "We all feel the weight of responsibility resting on our shoulders. On the other hand, I am confident that this mission will be possible if we join forces and act as one toward the common goal. I suggest that we go down to the deepest point of the city, where the master holding frame of the entire mechanism had been dislocated. We must put it back into its proper place before we can start any meaningful repair work on other areas."

Chapter Eleven

❦

Lilla Pitagon

Adrian and the thirteen Eagles were moving forward according to plan, so Lilla had an opportunity to strike up a conversation with her Pitagon guide. "Tell me something about yourself and your family," Lilla said to Lilla Pitagon.

The Pitagon nodded agreeably. "You should know some things about my life, especially the story of how I ended up among the Pitagons. It began in the old days, when I was roaming around with my three siblings after running away from home. We left our home because we got fed up with our father, who was out of a job for too long and did not take good care of us. At that time, we thought that he did not love any of us children. I remember that day so clearly. It's as if it happened yesterday, although it was a very long, long time ago …"

* * * * *

The wind blew sand into my eyes on the day we left home, and the clouds were hanging low up ahead of us. I told my siblings to hurry because it looked like it might start to rain. Peter, my little brother, asked why we couldn't wait until the weather was nicer to run away from home.

"Don't be silly!" I scolded him. "We have to hurry." I drew Peter and my sister, Mary, closer to me as we walked briskly down the road. I explained that we had no choice but to leave, even though we all felt bad about leaving our mother.

"But why must we go today?" Peter whined.

"I don't want to go today either!" protested my little sister, Mary.

"We have to leave now, because Father will be home soon, and I cannot bear another day of the suffering he imposes on us. Ever since he has been out of work, he is just not himself."

"You're right, Sis," Peter agreed reluctantly. "We'd better go! Tomorrow will be better when Daddy gets work, and then we can go back home."

I shook my head and said firmly, "No, Peter. We won't be coming back—not ever!"

The wind around us was growing stronger, and we could barely hold onto each other's arms, so we laced our fingers together to try to keep the wind from blowing us apart. Peter begged for us to go back home, but just at that moment, I saw my mother walking toward us from the next corner. She'd discovered we were gone and had come looking for us. Before she could reach us, a ferocious whirlwind touched down right next to us and lifted all of us up from the ground. I could see my mother watching in horror, and then she fell to her knees. "Dear God, don't do this to me!" she cried. "Please don't take my children from me!"

The wind was incredibly strong, and we could hear a deep roaring sound over our heads. The three of us held each other tightly, and suddenly, a bright blue light lifted us upward, even higher. I saw my mother painfully crying and begging, but the blue light embraced us and did not let go. We were all scared, but we didn't even dare to cry. I was so shaken that I shut my eyes in fear, and then I felt a warm, caressing feeling come over me as we were carried increasingly higher. Somehow, I felt relieved and happy, but then I thought about my mother again and how terrible she must feel. At that point, I was no longer able to see her. As I opened my eyes again, I saw that my siblings had their eyes shut tight, and tears were rolling down Mary's cheeks.

"Don't you cry, Mary!" I called to her. "Don't be afraid! Look at me and little Peter! We're not crying." For some reason, my voice rang out and echoed back to me in a very interesting tone. I occasionally opened my eyes again as we continued to rise higher, and I saw that we were standing inside an egg-shaped capsule with blue light gleaming from a metallic surface right below our feet. We all started shivering, though not from fright—the inside of the capsule had become chilly. But no sooner had we noticed the cold air than we felt the gentle rush of a warm breeze streaming from above and embracing all of us.

"I've changed my mind!" Mary cried. "I don't want to run away anymore." But we no longer had a choice.

It seemed like a long time, but we probably traveled for about six to eight minutes, and then I saw a flashing light getting closer to us. It emitted a hazy glow between its bright flashes. Soon, the bright egg-shaped capsule we were standing in came to an abrupt stop and opened up. We saw a tall young man—he must have been eight feet tall—in front of us. He had blond hair, and his eyes were as blue as the ocean. He wore gorgeous silver clothes that sparkled in a bluish haze. When the man looked at me, I could hear his thoughts inside my head.

"Poor, unfortunate children," he said. *"I will help you."* I looked around to see where we were and noticed we were standing in the middle of a large, circular room. Other people gathered around the man—they all were as tall as he was—and the man continued to communicate his thoughts through my mind. I was absolutely overwhelmed by his words.

"My friends and I are from another planet, called Kyara," he said in my head. *"We are here to help you. You children have a chance to live on Kyara, if you are deemed fit for that."* After that, the man started to speak out loud in our native language, so that my sister and brother could hear and understand him, too. He then called us forward, and as we stood there, motionless, we felt the warm brush of a breeze come over us again.

"You are receiving the warm caress of the breeze," he explained, "because you are still very young. We believe that loving care is essential to your development. It is a good thing that you are able to sense our embrace and affection—this is a sign that you are worthy to receive the gift of our great longevity." At this time, a different stranger stepped behind each one of us. "These are your Pitagons," he said. "They must take care of you and hold you accountable."

Suddenly, I decided I didn't like this turn of events, and I cried out that I wanted my mother. With that, the man turned to the others and proposed that they bring our parents aboard the ship. "No!" I cried out, surprising him. "Please do not do that. Even though we love our dad, he is a very difficult man with a bad temperament."

But the man just smiled and said, "Don't worry about that, child! We know exactly how to change him into a valuable person, such as a trained soldier."

After that, we followed the man, with the three Pitagons closely behind us. We walked through a maze of long corridors and passages for a long time, until we got to a dark doorway. There, the tall man turned around to face us.

"We've arrived at the transformation chamber," he told us. "You children will be converted into a different form, so please get ready and take your places." I saw three glass beds built into the walls, and as the tall man walked past them, the glass doors all opened up. He called to us, saying, "Come here, children, and lie down on these beds. The machine will put you to sleep, and after the program is completed, you will wake up again. When you sleep in these beds, you will be able to live more than 950 earthly years."

My sister, Mary, seemed eager to comply, but Peter and I hesitated. I didn't know whether we could trust this man, and I was really missing my mother. All three of us began to cry. The Pitagons didn't know what to do with us, so they started to cry, just like us, which took us by surprise.

"You stop crying and bring our mother here!" Mary said, still sobbing.

The Pitagons looked at each other, and whispered something that we couldn't understand. "We'll get your mom if you get in the beds," one said.

I was afraid it was a trick, so I refused. "Our mom always told us to be wary of strangers."

The tall man had watched this exchange with our Pitagons, and although he looked at us with a disapproving expression, I could see he was trying to hide a smile. He said, "All right, then. Come with me." Before we could do anything, we felt a warm breeze waft over us. Mary tried to resist the warmth and yelled at her Pitagon again to leave us alone.

The Pitagon just smiled and said, "This is our way of taking care of you and expressing affection."

Then the tall man told us again that we were to go with him. We walked back along the same series of hallways, following the tall man until we arrived at a gigantic red door, which immediately opened up as we approached it. We found ourselves in a large chamber with a beautiful domed ceiling, where a great number of people were working around large desks. We saw strange lights flashing along the walls and overhead, which made us stop and marvel at the beauty of this unique sight. I heard the relaxing tunes of pleasant music, and I noticed a gorgeous woman was standing far up on a stage, singing to this music.

At that time, I heard the man's voice again, in my head, telling me our parents would arrive soon. It angered me that he was inside my head again, and I told him so.

"Communicating telepathically is a much easier way to communicate," he told me. *"We have the ability to enter and read each other's thoughts at any time, even when the other is sleeping."*

I was hoping he'd help me look inside Mary's mind, but before I could ask, he called for the attention of our Pitagon guides and all the people who were working there. "I have an idea!" he said—by this time I'd figured out that he was the leader of the aliens. "Take the children to play on another planet that is similar to Earth but even more beautiful, where they can meet different creatures. You need to dazzle them and make them happy. Take good care of them, and bring them back safely in three days' time!"

Mary was excited that we were going somewhere to play. She

stared curiously at the Pitagons for a moment but then allowed her guide to take her hand and walk out with her. Peter was startled, and he pulled his hands away from his Pitagon. That was when he noticed something was shining in the Pitagon's hand.

"That's the control of my information system," the Pitagon explained.

We heard a slight whooshing sound as three travel spheres appeared overhead. They descended on us, and within a short time, I lost sight of my siblings. The sphere around me began to spin and lift off. At that moment, I closed my eyes and felt an incredible push as the sphere flew away at great speed. A few moments later, I opened my eyes, but only darkness surrounded me. I couldn't see my Pitagon guide, but I asked where we were going. I received no answer. We floated through the dark space for a long time that seemed like eternity. The pressure weighing on my body was unrelenting, and it tugged me down with robust force. I felt anxious and in need of help, so I called out desperately to my guide again, asking where we were going. I was surprised by the sound of my own voice, which had a strange, squeaky tone to it.

This time my Pitagon answered, "Don't talk right now! Our minds are traveling to another world that is even more enchanting than your Mother Earth. I control this journey within your thoughts, and that's how it becomes a reality." He assured me that my siblings would be there, too. "For now, you must stop talking," he cautioned me. "It might make you sick."

After that, I stayed silent, closed my eyes, and didn't even dare to twitch. I slowly felt the pressure on me letting up as our speed dropped off, and then everything became very bright. I opened my eyes and saw the sphere descending and touching the ground. We got out of the capsule, and soon after that, I spotted my siblings quite close by to the place where I landed. One of the other Pitagons called out to us to come take a look at the clear blue river. When Mary and Peter had gathered there with me, the Pitagon announced, "I can walk on water. Do you want me to show you?" Mary was eager to see him try this feat, but then he asked, "Do you want to walk on water with me?"

Mary glared at him and said, "Don't joke with me, alien! I'm not going with you. You go by yourself!"

The Pitagon smiled. "Just take my hand and think about walking on water."

Mary hesitated, but when Peter rushed to take the Pitagon's hand, she quickly grabbed the other hand, and I saw them leap onto the surface of the water. They didn't sink; they took careful steps that eventually took them farther and farther out until I lost sight of them altogether. I was left there, standing next to my Pitagon guide on the bank of an alien river on an alien planet.

My Pitagon asked, "Do you want to try walking on water, too?" But I just wanted to know where my brother and sister had gone, and I told him so. He seemed relieved. "I am very old, by the standards of the Earth," he explained, "and my gigantic abilities no longer work on this planet. At one time I could walk on water, but I haven't done it in ages." His face brightened as he told me, "I still know lots of things that could be fun and interesting. Ask me anything, and I will do my best to grant your wish! After all, that's why we are here—to have fun."

I got excited, and started thinking about what to wish for, but in the meantime, I could not escape my worry about the safety of my siblings. Finally, I told him, "I wish that I either could live four thousand years—but I don't want to look and feel old—or could stay young and live forever, until the world ends."

The Pitagon said, "Living for four thousand years doesn't sound like an impossible wish—you were chosen to receive a long life by transformation anyway—but I cannot promise you that you will live forever. Such an esteemed privilege has been granted to only one person so far. If that person can unravel the secret of immortality, then you might be able to share in that gift. In fact, once we unravel and discern the many details of this mystery, then all people will live for an eternity. Nothing will be able to harm them anymore."

"But won't there be too many people on Earth if everyone lives for all eternity?"

He answered me with firm assurance, "There is a lot of room on Earth and throughout the universe for people to live. Life is a wonderful thing, and every person has a right to live, and it is a duty to cherish life. Everyone must respect and protect the life of the other person as well as his own." Then he knelt down next to me, and his face brightened. "So did you decide what you want to play?" he asked me.

"I want to play life!" I told him with enthusiasm.

He smiled indulgently at me. "Actually, life should be lived, not played, even though you should live it playfully. And I think you already do that, so think of something else that would make you happy."

"Then let's go back where we came from!" I requested.

"So you don't even want to play?"

"I do," I said, "but not here."

"All right," he agreed. "Your wish is my command. From this day onward, I will serve as your personal guide and your teacher."

"Do you ... want to be my father too?" I asked quietly.

"No, I cannot be your father, but I would love to be your friend."

"I accept you as a friend, since I don't know anyone else on this planet."

He smiled again. "It looks like it's going to rain! We should look for cover!"

I looked around for a shelter but saw none. "Maybe you want to hide underground," I teased him.

He shook his head. "No, my friend, I'm going to teach you

how to travel on the train of thoughts in order to take shelter on another planet."

My eyes widened, partly in fear, partly in surprise. "But ... but I want ... I want to go back to where we came from!" I sputtered. "I want my brother and sister!"

The Pitagon only said, "Stand very close to me and hold my hand!"

I backed away slightly. His appearance was grotesque, and I didn't want to touch him. "Shouldn't we get going?" I asked. "Now it's raining!"

The Pitagon stood quietly, ignoring my reaction. Then he whispered, "Don't concentrate your thoughts on the rain."

"I'm not!" I insisted. "I'm thinking about the sphere taking us back where we came from."

"Concentrate harder! I need your help, because I'm too old and my thoughts often stray. By the way, I can teach you to live under water."

"What was that you just said about your thoughts straying?" I scoffed. "Anyway, I'd rather stay on dry land. Let's just go back!"

"Then here we go!"

"Yes, I want to go right now!" I demanded.

"We'll catch up to them soon, if we hurry up," the Pitagon suggested.

"Why didn't I just go with them in the first place?" I said, suddenly sobbing. The Pitagon was looking at me, and his eyes were filling up with tears. "Can you cry, too?" I asked him in surprise.

"Indeed I can. If you cry, then I cry too."

"Don't cry!" I begged him. "I will stop crying, too!"

We agreed, and that created a friendship bond between us—and we set out to find my brother and sister. A travel sphere descended on us again, and we flew swiftly upon the train of thoughts after my siblings.

"What are you thinking about?" the Pitagon called out to me. "The sphere is spinning wildly out of control!"

"I imagined myself at a state fair, sitting on a carousel with my brother and sister, and we are spinning around and around."

The Pitagon clenched his teeth, not attempting to hide his disapproval. "*Why* are you thinking about that when you are supposed to focus on finding the path of your siblings?" he fumed. "We are not on the right track because of your wandering thoughts. We will never find them like this! Both of us must concentrate hard, so the travel sphere can put us on the right path."

"Are you sure that we can think about the same thing at the same time?" I asked meekly.

The Pitagon exhaled slowly as he smiled at my remark. I saw a sense of joy coming over him, because he could tell that I no longer saw him as an enemy. "We can do it, so let's begin now!" he said. "It will get dark, but don't be afraid; I will be right here with you, so take my hand." He extended his hand toward me; it looked gray, and his fingers were long and wrinkly with overgrown fingernails. A shiny circle glowed green in the palm of his hand, with alternating red flashes. I pulled my hand away, so he wouldn't be able to touch me. He looked at me with a puzzled expression on his face.

"I don't want to touch you!" I shouted, suddenly afraid again.

"Fine, I promise that I won't touch you, but remember that I'm here for you if you get scared."

"It's … it's enough for me to know that you are here with me," I told him.

"The sphere will not work properly until both of us are focusing on the same thoughts," he snapped at me.

"I can't tell what you are thinking!" I complained. "Why can't you teach me your ways? It would be easier if I could read minds, too!"

"I could teach you that skill, but I would have to enter your mind and take control of it, and before that, you will need to learn obedience. I have been respectful enough not to wander into your mind, but it will be absolutely necessary for me to do so in this process."

"Just get us out of here before it's too late," I said. "Can't you see that the storm is here?"

After that, I obeyed the Pitagon, even though my knees were shaking. I felt that we were rushing forth in space with incredible velocity, but to where, I had no idea. The Pitagon's thoughts were powerfully directing my mind, and I rapidly gained the skills of thought control and how to enter someone's mind unnoticed. The physical pressure on me was again so overwhelming that I started becoming disoriented, and I have no memory of the following minutes, hours, or days. When I regained consciousness, I found myself aboard the alien spaceship again, heading for a new world, where I would spend the next two thousand years of my life.

I lived the first 950 years as a chosen human in a converted form. After that, I became a Pitagon, just like my guide. He was three thousand years old at the time when he handed over his energy and knowledge to me. One day, not long after I arrived in the new world, I saw him tottering, and I ran over to him, trying to help, but there was nothing I could do. As I held him in my arms, I suddenly sensed his energy rushing into me as his body crumbled into ashes.

*   *   *   *   *

Lilla Pitagon sighed heavily, as if retelling her tale had exhausted her physically. Finally, when she spoke again, her voice seemed rather small. "I never found my siblings or either of my parents. My journey took me to a whole different world, and to my knowledge, my brother and sister were in another dimension. Perhaps I'll set out to search for them again one day," she finished hopefully.

"Thank you for telling me your fascinating story," said Lilla.

"I'm surprised you could remember your childhood memories, especially in such great detail."

"Memories may fade, but they never are forgotten," the Pitagon replied. "They help invigorate the soul and bring happiness with every joyful image of the good old days. It is very important to hold on to the good and sort through everything else. My memories live on within my heart, and they will never be lost. However, I don't spend time in the past; I live for the present, and that's the way it should be."

"I agree with that!" Lilla said enthusiastically. "It's quite normal to put aside the past and bring the memories back only when you want to remember."

Adrian had been sitting silently through Lilla Pitagon's long story. Now, he felt he needed to add his opinion. "Your job is important, Lilla," he said. "As long as you keep occupied with the present, you don't have time to reminisce about the past. You are all grown up now, so looking ahead should be the most important thing for you, just like it is for me."

Chapter Twelve

>-·-◆-·-O-·-◆-·-◄

The Third Dimension

Lilla pressed her face against the windscreen of the spaceship and looked out into the darkness. "I wonder where we are right now," she said.

"It's not clear what this place is," Adrian answered, "but our Pitagon guides are keeping a close eye on our ship's path. I wonder whether they follow it telepathically or actually provide physical directions to our Eagles."

"Should we try to hear their thoughts?" Lilla asked.

"Go on and try it," Adrian encouraged her. "Actually, we both should try it at the same time."

"Good idea," Lilla agreed. "Try to enter Lilla Pitagon's mind, and see how she reacts."

"No, I'd rather try Adrian Pitagon. Lilla Pitagon is your protector."

"Why don't we do the way they do? They linger in our minds all the time."

"I don't think they are doing that all the time," Adrian countered. "I'm sure their minds are far away now, dealing with more important things right now, or learning skills that may come in handy later on. That's why they always seem to know everything."

"You could be right," Lilla said. "I've been watching their faces. They do look like they're far away from this place."

Adrian narrowed his eyes as he looked at the Pitagons. "Perhaps we could find out for sure if we said something to them. If we talk, they'll notice us."

Lilla shook her head impatiently. "No, don't say anything! Just enter their minds already!"

"All right," Adrian said, nodding, but then he hesitated. "You don't suppose ... do you think our Pitagons were scanning our minds as we were talking?"

Lilla sighed heavily and threw up her hands in exasperation. "You haven't been paying attention. They are preoccupied with something else right now!"

"Am I clear to do this then?" Adrian asked, still unsure of whether he should attempt to read his Pitagon's mind.

"Yes, you are!" Lilla hissed at him. "Come *on*! I'm already reading Lilla Pitagon's thoughts."

"Okay, I'll just let you—"

"Adrian!" Lilla interrupted suddenly. "We have a problem! Lilla Pitagon has led the Eagles into the third dimension."

"You're not serious!" Adrian uttered in disbelief.

"I *am* serious!" Lilla assured him. She shook her head slightly, as if trying to clear her own thoughts. "Adrian, what should we do?"

"We have to stop them!" Adrian said determinedly. "We need answers from them!"

"But how?" Lilla wailed. What had seemed such fun just moments ago—practicing entering her Pitagon's head—had turned suddenly sour.

"We have to be careful not to stall them too suddenly," Adrian advised. "It might be dangerous. We need a good plan."

"What if we sneak into the deepest part of their minds and slow them down?" Lilla suggested.

Adrian shrugged helplessly. "Let's try it! I hope we're doing the right thing."

Lilla's thoughts were soaring so fast that she could hardly keep up. Finally, she was able to successfully access the Pitagon's deepest thoughts.

"*I'm completely lost!*" Lilla Pitagon cried out in her head.

"*All of us are lost!*" communicated Lilla.

"*Why are you so deep into my mind?*" Lilla Pitagon asked, Even in her head, the Pitagon's tone was one of annoyance.

"*I think you know that very well!*" Lilla retorted.

Lilla Pitagon snorted derisively. "*You won't be able to reset our course, and I certainly refuse to do it.*"

"*Turn the Eagles back,*" Lilla ordered, with new resolve. "*We must return to our original mission!*"

Lilla Pitagon's tone abruptly changed; now she wheedled, *"You should be trying to give us strength to find my siblings! I can feel their presence really close by."*

"No, this will get us into trouble," Lilla warned.

"A little detour won't hurt," the Pitagon insisted. *"I just want to see my siblings once more!"*

"Jupiter entrusted you to take care of me to your care, and you just wander off?" Lilla said accusingly.

"I didn't go alone," Lilla Pitagon said. *"Adrian Pitagon is my helper, as are the other eleven Eagles."*

Completely exasperated by her Pitagon's unwillingness to listen, Lilla said petulantly, *"I'm going to tell on you to Jupiter!"*

"Don't be silly, little girl," the Pitagon scolded. *"Now stop pestering me. I can feel my siblings are near; I've been feeling it for a long time."*

Lilla sat back for a moment, unsure of what to do next. She was fearful of the third dimension but she was at a loss as to how to deal with this Pitagon. Finally, she spoke to Lilla Pitagon again in her mind. *"Would you still recognize your siblings if you talked to them in person?"*

"I think that I would," the Pitagon responded.

"Then tell Adrian to find a safe place to land in this dimension. You're going to meet with each Pitagon to see if you recognize your siblings. If you find them, then we can quickly resume our voyage."

"I will do as you say!" the Pitagon agreed. *"Let me communicate to Adrian's mind."*

"I'm already here in your mind," Adrian said. *"And I've read your thoughts. We are not landing in this dimension because we have to resume our trip. Give me the coordinates so the Eagles can find their way back."*

The Pitagon was silent for a moment and then said quietly, *"I don't remember."*

"Just try!" Adrian demanded.

"I'm old," Lilla Pitagon whined. *"It's not easy. Besides … I didn't think that a small detour was such a big problem."*

"You're outrageous!" Adrian stormed through her mind. He paced back and forth on the ship, as he grasped the gravity of the situation that Lilla Pitagon and Adrian Pitagon had caused. "I have to stop them," he said aloud to no one in particular. "Earth is in danger." Then he turned to Lilla. "We're on a mission, yet end up in another dimension. How could this happen?"

"They do seem to play around like children," Lilla said patiently. "Perhaps that's the secret to their legendary longevity—a lively spirit."

"You are thinking correctly, my friend," Lilla Pitagon spoke to both of their minds. *"Life requires a lot of patience—and playfulness. Being in good spirits is truly the secret to a long and healthy life. That keeps your body calm and free of trouble. But never fear—there is one way to quickly find our way back."*

"I'm ordering you to immediately command the Eagle ships with your mind," Adrian sputtered, "and get them back on their original course. Do it now, because we are behind schedule!"

"What do you mean, behind schedule?" Lilla Pitagon's voice came sweetly to his mind. *"We cannot ever be late, because my thought control can put us back on track in just one leap."*

"This is to all Eagles!" Adrian shouted, issuing the command. "I'm commanding you to initiate amplification for thought transfer!"

At that moment, another Pitagon spoke from one of the Eagle ships. "We copy and stand ready to fulfill your command! However, please allow my brother and me to transport over to your ship. We believe that your Pitagon guide is our lost sister. We ask you to please accept us!"

Adrian and Lilla listened in astonishment to the Pitagon's request. Lilla nodded to Adrian, who then said, "I'm granting permission for you to come aboard the mother ship, if Lilla Pitagon is indeed your sister."

The two smaller Eagle ships began their approach to the mother ship, and soon the gates opened before them, letting the three siblings greet each other as Pitagons. Their eyes overflowed with tears, but they were tears of joy. It was hard for anyone to tell them apart, as all three of them looked very much alike. In witnessing their joyous reunion, Adrian realized that no matter where someone is in the world, the bond created by family relationships can never be broken. Siblings might not keep in touch for a period of time, but the yearning created by love that ties a family together will always pull siblings back to each other, allowing them to find one another again after many years of separation. The new Pitagons gave their names as Mary Pitagon and Peter Pitagon.

Lilla Pitagon wiped her eyes as she released her siblings from her embrace. She squared her shoulders and became quite business-like again. "Now, we have to start heading back to our original dimension," she told them. "We must save the human race on Earth, which will provide the basis to our longevity."

"It's important for all of us to concentrate together in order to navigate our ships back," said Adrian. He lifted both of his arms and turned toward the Pitagons.

"Stop!" Lilla Pitagon cried. "Don't hurt us! We are loyal and dedicated Pitagons. We are only playful in order to make our long lives more fun. Otherwise, think how boring our extremely long lives would be!"

Adrian sighed heavily. "Why do you think ill of me right away?" he questioned.

"I thought that you wanted to use your power to discipline us," Lilla Pitagon answered sheepishly.

"I wouldn't do that," Adrian assured her. "I've never hurt anyone in my life. I only use my power to help me fulfill my duty and to defend myself but never against you, my friends."

"I'm relieved to hear your words," Lilla Pitagon answered. "Then, it's time to begin our concentration in order to safely leave this dimension."

Adrian extended his arms at shoulder level, with his palms turned toward the Pitagons. His power streamed from his palms, creating a glowing blue light beam that surrounded the Pitagons. As he stood there, exuding his power, a red star appeared on Adrian's forehead that also beamed brightly onto the Pitagons. Lilla watched the event in amazement as the Eagles burst out of the third dimension at an enormous speed. The ships quickly dropped into another dimension, and they found themselves on Earth, landing on vast fields of corn in the state of Texas. It was a clear, crisp evening, and the Eagle ships lit up the entire field.

A farmhouse stood near the edge of one of the cornfields, and an elderly couple sat outside on the front porch, watching the sky. They couldn't have missed the strange lights of the Eagles descending on their property.

Lilla Pitagon and Adrian Pitagon exited their ship and walked straight to the front porch of the house. They clearly heard the old couple talking to each other.

"Do you see this, Susie?" the old man asked. "Those … creatures are coming right up to us."

"What are they, Johnny?" the old woman asked. "Midgets?"

The two Pitagons raised up their right arms and turned their palms toward the elderly couple.

"What do you suppose they want?" the old woman whispered, edging closer to her husband.

"I don't know," he said softly, not taking his eyes from the Pitagons, "but I'm sure not going to ask."

The Pitagons smiled as they stood firmly in front of the old couple, illuminating the porch with the light streaming from their hands.

"Johnny, go on and ask them something," the old woman urged. "Ask them why they came here!"

The old man sat up as erect as possible in his rocker. He cleared his throat loudly and then shouted at the Pitagons, "What are you doing on my property?"

Lilla Pitagon smiled at the old man and said plainly, "We came here to fix your sore back."

The old man's eyes narrowed as he stared suspiciously at the Pitagons. "The local doctors already gave up on fixing me," he said. "How do you propose to fix it?"

In response, the two Pitagons stepped forward and directed their energies—in the form of glowing red light beams—toward the old man's lower back. A couple of seconds later, he sprang up from his chair and turned to his elderly wife with a youthful step.

"I can't believe this! Just this morning, I was aching all over, and I couldn't sit comfortably in my chair," the old man rejoiced.

"John, you seem in better shape than ever!" his wife observed. "Lord knows that I'd love to get out of this chair too, but I'm scared to stand up. I might pinch a nerve."

John turned to the Pitagons to plead with them. "Won't you do something for my wife?"

The Pitagons nodded and focused their power toward the old woman. In the blink of an eye, she hopped up from her chair with great ease. She stared at the Pitagons in awe, whispering, "Thank you. How can I thank you?"

"You don't need to thank us," Lilla Pitagon said, "and you don't have to die just because you've gotten old. You could come with us instead. As chosen people, you may regain your youth."

"That's great," the old man said, speaking for both of them. "We're ready to follow you to the end of this world!" Then he looked over at his wife. "Right, Susie?"

The old woman nodded enthusiastically. "If we can be young and free of pain, we will go with you."

The couple had just walked down from their porch, ready to join the Pitagons, when Adrian and Lilla appeared behind them. Lilla Pitagon was tremendously worried when she noticed that the ruby crystal in the palm of Adrian's hand was blazing, its light shining so brightly that it flooded the entire farmhouse. "I sense a storm raging inside your mind," Lilla Pitagon said nervously. "The crystal in your hand gave it away. Did something happen?"

"It's nothing bad," Adrian assured her. "I'm not here to discipline you. I'm just having a hard time focusing my thoughts, so I'm not about to let my power loose. This beaming light won't harm you; it's simply honoring your hard work."

"Oh, boy! I knew that you couldn't yet handle the power you received!" said Adrian Pitagon.

"I certainly can handle it," Adrian insisted. "You'll see. I will now project part of my power in the form of light energy over to all of you who are present," Adrian stated. "This will help us penetrate the powerful walls of the lost dimension. Have no fear—the ruby crystal provides enough force to protect all of you from death and will allow us to safely pass through, completely unharmed."

"Are you saying that we are not on planet Earth?" asked Lilla Pitagon.

"No, we aren't. It's very similar, but it isn't the Earth."

"Whose fault it that?" Adrian Pitagon asked. "What could be the cause of this?"

"For one thing, I know that you Pitagons have wandering minds," Adrian explained. "One of you probably didn't focus on the original Earth, and that person must have been stronger than those of us who *were* focusing on Earth. I can't even identify this dimension. I have no idea where we are."

"I know where we are! We're at the right place!" disputed Lilla Pitagon.

"No, we definitely are not!" Adrian said firmly. "This is a home of a farmer, and we should get out of here in a hurry!"

"Not so fast!" Lilla Pitagon said, looking toward the old man and his wife. "These two people here need to go with us."

Adrian scowled and glanced over at the couple, who stood with mouths agape at this strange meeting. "What are you talking about?" he demanded to know.

"We've got to bring them along to brighten our days!" Lilla Pitagon insisted.

"I'm the captain of the Eagle ships!" exclaimed Adrian. "I'm responsible for everything and everybody."

"I know that, but I'm a two-thousand-year-old Pitagon called Lilla Pitagon, and just so you know, I specifically wanted to come here. I was the one that ordered this special mission for myself and everyone else!"

Adrian took a long step forward and placed himself inches from Lilla Pitagon so she would be certain to see the displeasure written on his face. "You deserve to be punished for this, you unruly old Pitagon! You constantly cause problems, whether you pretend to be sick, joke around to confuse us, or knowingly put us on the wrong path."

"That's how you can learn so much from me," Lilla Pitagon said sweetly.

The elderly couple stood perfectly still, both wearing puzzled expressions, but the old man felt the urge to interject with a remark. "I sure hope you gentlemen won't leave us here."

Lilla Pitagon smiled warmly at the pair. "The two of you can certainly come with us."

"We're going!" John replied and then quickly added, "I just hope your captain doesn't have any objections."

"I won't—as long as you behave yourselves," answered Adrian. "Anyway, you're chosen humans, even if you're not from our planet Earth."

"Are you saying that there is another Earth?" John asked.

Adrian nodded. "There might even be more! They could be bigger or smaller and some may not even be in a different dimension but right here within the solar system."

John and Susanne headed toward the spaceship in high spirits. "Oh, Johnny, this is fantastic!" Susanne gushed. "We're not only strong again, but we're also about to travel the world!"

"Keep quiet!" John hissed. "There's no way to know what might offend these aliens. I don't want them to decide to leave us here."

Susanne nodded silently, and in the next moment, two travel spheres lowered onto them and whisked them away to the Eagle mother ship. The Pitagons were already in position aboard the ship, awaiting the two new arrivals. Adrian greeted the couple warmly as the travel spheres dropped away from them. "Welcome to our Eagle mother ship! This will take us to our correct destination."

"Are you the big boss?" inquired John.

"I'm the commander of the fleet of these thirteen Eagle ships," Adrian responded. "I am allowing you to come with us to our Earth. Let's just hope we can successfully break out of this dimension." He motioned for Lilla Pitagon to step forward as he said to the couple, "You need to take a seat now. Your safety is an important concern, as gravitational forces might rattle our ship."

"Let me assist you," Lilla Pitagon said. "Follow me." She led them to their seats and helped them buckle their seatbelts, all the while explaining, "Two of our new Pitagons will serve you for the rest of your lives. They are my long-lost siblings, and we just found each other recently. I'm overjoyed to have them here with us." At that moment, the two new Pitagons came on board and approached the newly arrived couple but did not speak.

In a few minutes, the Eagles headed off toward the correct dimension—their original destination. Adrian held out his hand, and the ruby crystal immediately started glowing again. Its force rushed through the entire ship. He then commanded his crew, saying, "Attention, all Pitagons of this fleet! I need your full focus in accomplishing our task! We must navigate our ships with coordinated thought transfer in order to reach the appropriate dimension of our Earth."

He swerved his arm, and the force of the dazzling light radiating from the crystal inside his hand passed over the passengers of the ship once more. It touched every one of them, and within a split second, they tore through space, into the other dimension.

Chapter Thirteen

>-+-⊹-+-○-+-⊹-+-<

Underwater City

"We have arrived!" rejoiced Lilla Pitagon, clapping her hands, and everyone else on board soon followed with applause as well. They were happy to have successfully broken out of the other dimension. The ruby crystal in Adrian's hand faded out and then went dark before it rapidly melted into his hand, blending in perfectly with his skin.

Seconds later, something lit up on Adrian's forehead. The light formed the shape of a pentacle, and this time its striking radiance was not red but pure white. Everyone noticed it, and their eyes became fixed on the strange sight.

"I can feel everyone's eyes on me," Adrian said, somewhat uncomfortably. "Why is that so?"

"You probably should be aware," said Adrian Pitagon with a smile, "that with the help of the ruby crystal, you seem to have acquired immortality from the third dimension. You're the only one in this world who has it—it's obvious from the pentacle shining on your forehead. The challenge for you will be to learn how to keep this matter an absolute secret—not an easy task when that star can appear on your forehead."

Adrian's hands flew to his forehead, as if to feel for the pentacle. "How can this be?" he mumbled in utter astonishment.

"From this day forward, you will possess a kind of immortality that only you can confer onto future generations," Adrian Pitagon explained. "You must learn to wield this power wisely, or you won't be able to pass it on to the rest of mankind. This blessing, however, might put you in grave danger, as there always will be people that will want to take this away from you. They might torture you to force you to hand over your immortality. If they succeed, then you will be doomed. Always be careful!"

Adrian nodded solemnly. "Of course I'll be careful," he promised, looking earnestly into Adrian Pitagon's eyes. Suddenly, he gasped. In Adrian Pitagon's eyes he saw his own mother and father, flying toward Washington DC. "Why are you showing me this?"

"We must not let emotions endanger the assignment we were entrusted with," the Pitagon told him.

"Why are they heading to the National Security Council?"

"We spent too much time in the other dimensions. Jupiter thought we were lost, so he decided to assign your parents to this job."

Adrian sighed resignedly. "All right, but what's our new assignment then?"

"We're going back to the underwater city to assist with the lifting process. With the power you possess, we can surely fix the problem."

"That sounds like an excellent challenge, but I'm worried about my parents and what might happen to them if the earthly humans attack them."

Adrian Pitagon immediately waved off Adrian's concern. "We would rush to their aid at once and rescue them, of course."

The groundwork of the lifting process was well underway in the underwater city. Frank Sr. and his friend Joe, a remarkable scientist, both labored on this project with great enthusiasm. The thirteen Eagles returned to their home docking stations, while the Pitagons and some of the other passengers headed to the Great Hall.

Adrian and Lilla got involved in the work of the city's lifting project.

"I'd like to know the proportionate size of the city's diameter," Adrian stated.

"The city is truly colossal; its sides reach all the way to the coasts," Lilla Pitagon answered.

"Will the seawater flood the coastal areas during the lifting process?"

"Such incidents will not be significant if the city rises out slowly. The water will just recede into the hollow cavity as the lifting project progresses. Once it's completed, the city will look as if it's floating on the surface, even though a gigantic, powerful arm will hold it up. This arm is the damaged area that requires repair now."

"I see. What does the city's exterior look like?" Adrian asked.

"It looks like a sphere made of crystal glass, with a steel holding arm. We brought special crystal from alien planets, so the city's outer shell is actually alive, and it's impossible to destroy. When the city emerges onto the surface, it shines with a golden splendor, and then it pulls down its protective shield to protect it from the effects of outside temperatures and the sun's energy as an invisible protection net is activated. It has the capability to protect itself against any weapon or other threat, rendering it virtually indestructible. The city can basically determine the source of a particular threat, and then it pulls that threat into the defensive net before sending it back to its origin at high velocity."

Adrian thought for a moment about what Adrian Pitagon had told him, but he had a concern of a different nature.
"I'd like to hear from my parents," he said. "I need to know how they are getting along."

Adrian Pitagon shook his head and said, not unkindly, "You'll have to be patient for a little while longer."

Chapter Fourteen

> ⊱ ⊰ ⊱ ○ ⊰ ⊱ ⊰

Rescue

Todd stepped into the Great Hall, followed by his entourage, and everyone stood up to bow toward them. Todd and his escorts greeted members of the assembly with a bow before he spoke to the gathering. "The time has come for us to act," he said in a loud, clear voice. "The leader of the National Security Council has arrested our special envoys because he believed them to be hostile aliens. Our chosen representatives underwent multiple transformations, and due to an unfortunate error, their bodies reversed to the converted form during negotiations, which resulted in their imprisonment. Their two Pitagon guides tried to set them free, but they were captured as well. I'm here to ask for Pitagon volunteers to rescue all of them from captivity on the wings of thought."

To this request, every single Pitagon in the room stepped forward to volunteer, but Todd waved them down with his words. "Thank you, thank you, my friends, but we only need ten Pitagons for this job."

Ten disciplined Pitagons were chosen, and in the blink of an eye they disappeared from the city. They almost instantly appeared inside the holding cells of the detainees and encircled them before applying focused light energy to open the cell doors. They all ran toward the exit, but there, the group encountered significant security presence. All Pitagons had to extend their arms to cast their combined energies upon the guards—this was in the form of a strong yellow light beam. The force of the beam was so powerful that it immediately pushed the guards aside, giving the group a clear way out. They encountered another problem, however, when they came upon the hundreds of people blocking the prison gates; the crowd had gathered just outside upon hearing the strange news of captured aliens. The Pitagons surrounded Frank Jr. and Emma to shield them from the people but they couldn't shield them from the comments.

"The end is near for all adulterers! The days of sin and torture are over! The Lord has arrived to bring punishment!"

"Those are alien creatures!"

"How did they get here? What do they use for space travel?"

The crowd pressed forward and pushed against the Pitagons, forcing them closer together with Frank and Emma. Then they heard a roaring sound. A blue light sphere swooped down onto the small group, quickly swallowing it up. With a flash of light they rapidly soared upward and soon found themselves aboard the mother ship. The crowd on the ground stood petrified, staring up to the sky in an attempt to see the aliens but were not able to spot anything.

"The miracle has manifested itself!" someone shouted from the crowd.

"Aliens do exist after all!" yelled another.

The Eagles returned to the underwater city, where the work continued. Emma and Frank joyfully embraced their son, and they also reunited with Grandfather Frank and Joe. "Oh, dear God, Dad—is that you?" Frank whispered incredulously, looking at his father.

"I hope you still remember me," Frank Sr. said. They looked joyfully at each other with their renewed strength and their rejuvenated forms.

"I was only a little boy the last time I saw you like this."

"It's a great joy to have grown and become young again," Frank Sr. said. "My buddy Joe looks even better than I do— young, strong, and stout, just like when he was twenty."

Soon afterward, Todd arrived in the hall again, and the Pitagons rushed back to their stations to continue their tasks. Emma and Frank went before Todd and told the sad story of their failed mission. Then Todd made another announcement.

"Even though earthly humans often rush to wrong conclusions, we still need to be persistent," he told the entire assembly gathered in the hall. "And we must do everything to save mankind. Earthly humans do not believe us; therefore, scores of innocent people will die before we can achieve our goal. It will be up to us to notify all humans as fast as possible of what is about to happen to Earth. We have to send a message to each and every person. In order to do this, we must take control of every radio and television station on the planet, so that every single source of information will broadcast our message. Simultaneously, we must begin the evacuation of people onto our mother ships stationed near Earth. It also will be our task to send volunteer Pitagons to any remote areas of Earth in order to locate those disadvantaged people who have no way of receiving our messages but are able to serve as chosen humans." Todd waved to the crowd and left the underwater city with his entourage.

The elderly couple, Susanne and John, stood close to Mary Pitagon and Peter Pitagon, but no one paid any attention to them. Everyone seemed to be too busy because of all the recent commotion.

Chapter Fifteen

>⊹⟨⟩⊹○⊹⟨⟩⊹<

The Anguish of Susanne and John

"Susie, do you think they've forgotten about the promise they made about making us young again?" John asked his wife.

"They must've forgotten about us," Susanne said forlornly. "What should we do to attract their attention?"

"You don't have to do anything," said Mary Pitagon. "I will intervene on your behalf … but I cannot do that just yet. Please be patient."

Lilla Pitagon approached them and glared at John and Susanne. "Please keep your voices down," she said sternly.

"It looks like we can only whisper around here," John told his wife. "Let's find a place where we can chat without being scolded." With that, they headed to find an available work station in the Great Hall.

"Keep your eyes open, John. You might learn something useful!" instructed Peter Pitagon.

"How could I benefit from any of this?" John grumbled. "This is a new world with new people and new dangers."

"Don't think of it that way," Peter Pitagon said encouragingly.

"There's one thing I can think of that I might need," John said. "Tell me … are families around here?"

"Absolutely, there are lots of them."

"How about priests?" John asked.

"There are priests as well," Peter Pitagon answered.

"Is there a Pope?"

"There's one Pope in this world," Peter Pitagon said, "but the seat of the Pope is in Rome."

"I must find him and talk to him!" John insisted.

Peter Pitagon was growing impatient with John. "What would you possibly want from the Pope of this world?" he scoffed.

"I want to request a new marital law—to allow men to marry as many times as they wish! Wouldn't that be progress?"

Adrian's boisterous approach immediately silenced them. "I overheard your conversation," Adrian said. "That's a brilliant idea, but it won't be an easy thing to carry out."

"Adrian, my leader," John said, "could you tell me why?"

"The Pope is not yet twenty years old, and he isn't married. Besides that, he is bound by ancient laws and traditions passed by his predecessors."

"Then let's capture the Pope," John suggested, "and transform him in the same way you did with my wife, Susanne, and me. We could convince him to get rid of this outdated law, and find a more appropriate solution that would be fair to all men."

"You haven't been fully transformed yet!" Adrian observed. "You don't completely understand the process. Problems might occur during the conversion—this happened with my own parents. Several conversion chambers exist, but the most developed one is on board the Eagle mother ship."

John seemed to grow agitated and instead of responding to Adrian, he turned on his wife, Susanne. "Don't you see that we don't belong together anymore? This is a completely different place. I just want to start a new life with a new wife!" He looked back at Adrian and said angrily, "So, you're some kind of leader. Can't you arrange for things like this? Or should I try to get the Pitagons to run off with me, and together we will abduct the Pope from Rome?"

Adrian sighed heavily, thoroughly perturbed by this man's behavior. "In the first place," he said slowly, as if he were speaking to a small child, "I'm not actually a leader in this place. I only lead on special missions. In the second place, you can't be serious about kidnapping the Pope."

"But this is only one small thing I want him to erase from this world—only one misguided law that binds people."

"The idea itself isn't a bad one," Lilla Pitagon interjected.

"No, you can't do this!" Adrian argued. "Marriage is a sacred thing. I urge you to think it through before you do anything."

"There's nothing to think about," John insisted. "It must be erased, and the Pope is the only person who can do this."

Adrian sighed again, frustrated with getting nowhere. "There's no need to abduct him, though; you can file a petition."

"Pushing paper won't do a thing!" John said adamantly. "We have to abduct him so he can be transformed, so he can think and feel the way we do."

"Nonsense. There won't be any kidnapping!" Adrian ordered. He turned to the Pitagons. "Take our guests from the other dimension immediately to the conversion chamber. Their minds need to be cleansed of these wrong ideas. Bring them back as calm and honest souls." Adrian lifted his hands, and the ruby crystal glowed toward the Pitagons and the elderly couple. Then he issued his command. "My power hereby removes every ill thought from all of you."

"Why would you change us?" cried out Adrian Pitagon.

"Your minds have wandered quite a bit lately and produced too many dishonest thoughts and explored dangerous new ways, which got us into a lot of trouble—but no more!" The bright red glow of energy suddenly turned to blue and completely spilled onto John, Susanne, and the two Pitagons. The energy rapidly spun around them, as an Eagle ship rolled in with massive speed and directed the misbehaving bunch to come aboard. Then the ship vanished with them, as fast as it had appeared.

Chapter Sixteen

➤⊰⊹⊶⊙⊷⊹⊱⊰

The Fall of Demon Pitagons

Once the ship was out of sight, Adrian seemed visibly relieved. "At last we can make some progress," he said, "except I no longer have a guide to assist me."

"I would be glad to serve as your aide," offered Peter Pitagon.

"Thank you, I accept your offer. First, however, I need to scan your mind to determine whether you are suitable."

"I'm sure I'm the best one for this job," Peter Pitagon said confidently. "I'm perfectly suitable."

Adrian held up his hand. "Sorry, but it seems that you're actually not. You don't possess the same values as we do here on Earth, which will lead to serious conflicts. For this reason, you and your sibling will be sent into exile and return to the dimension you came from. Otherwise, my power will destroy you."

"We can't go back!" the Pitagons shouted.

Adrian shrugged. "Then I'll have to use my power." As soon as Adrian lifted his arm, the ruby crystal in his hand lit up again, and its fierce light beam encircled the Pitagons. In a matter of seconds, Peter Pitagon and Mary Pitagon turned into ancient people. The changeover revealed their true evil faces, and both of them began shouting out threats.

"We'll be back, and we'll take the power of immortality from you! We will destroy you!"

No matter how much the Pitagons resisted, they were not able to overcome the awesome force. Within a few minutes, the two deceitful Pitagons were reduced to pieces of glowing cinder that then quickly turned into ashes. Adrian could hear the sounds of distant screams, while the sky hurled down a series of powerful lightning strikes—the strikes were so massive that they seemed to hit everywhere.

Adrian never flinched as the screams sounded and the lightning struck around him. "Today ..." he said slowly, "I killed two demons."

All of the people and the Pitagons present in the hall stood up and applauded his courageous accomplishment. A sad feeling came over Adrian, although he couldn't fully grasp the meaning of it, as his actions were controlled primarily by his power and his instincts.

Lilla tried to comfort him. "You don't have to be sad."

"I can't believe I lost two of my most sensible, measured,

and honest Pitagons due to the bad influence from the corrupt dimension. They were swayed by the thoughts of Lilla Pitagon's siblings. I hope that our dear guides will soon return to us, fully recovered."

"I hope for the best, too." Todd said as he stepped onto the scene. "I made arrangements for the rehabilitation of your two kind-hearted Pitagons. As for the chosen people, John and Susanne, I ordered a full investigation to make sure they won't return here if they're also found to be corrupted."

"Thank you for your help," Adrian responded.

"Team work can only be good!" Todd said. "Now, my dear children, let's get back to our task as soon as possible, because the threat to Earth is imminent. Let's give humanity a chance for survival. We must save this pure race of humans in order to save ourselves."

Adrian turned toward the Pitagons and people present in the Great Hall. "In order to do that, we have to get close to them and telepathically guide them to the right path."

Chapter Seventeen

⊱┤◈•○•◈┤⊰

Complication on Earth

The eldest Pitagons and the eldest chosen humans walked to the massive roundtable in the center of the hall. There were exactly 124 Pitagons and an equal number of humans present, and one by one, they all stepped up to the table. They remained standing, with their eyes fixed forward. The roundtable itself actually was a huge brain-machine, which was equipped with a large processor unit that boasted a vast capacity. They needed all the power of this machine to assist them with their colossal task.

A projection appeared in the center that showed all of the enormous laser-drawn collection circles that were beamed down to several different places on Earth from the Eagle mother ship out in space. Inside the collection circles were smaller rings that served to transport people, and each of these rings actually was an egg-shaped travel sphere. The people living near the large laser circles immediately noticed the arrival of these strange spheres, and the news quickly spread around the globe. Upon hearing the news, people congregated in large numbers around each of these sights. Their faces showed signs of the fear that filled their hearts. Women and children cried, while men just stared in shock, and they all felt the weight of their helplessness pressing down on them. People saw their lives pass before their eyes, and they knew that they would have to answer for their missteps and mistakes. There seemed to be no other choice but to accept that this opportunity offered by their ancestors, the Pitagons, was the last chance for survival. There was no other way out, yet nobody dared to be the first one to step inside the circle.

At that point, everyone around the brain-machine began to focus their attention on the cities of New York City, Washington DC, and Miami, as the crowds in those places started to kneel down in prayer. Young or old, they all began to sing as one. Those gathered around the brain-machine recognized the song as Psalms 23:1. "The Lord is my shepherd, I shall not want." People all around the world carried on singing religious songs, day and night. Crowds stood up and started singing Psalm 90 of the Genevan Psalter. "Lord, you have been our dwelling place in all generations." Still, no one moved, and crowds continued to wait in anticipation for something or somebody. In the distance, men dressed in black and wearing black hats approached the crowd, forced their way through the people, and headed straight to the circle. Each of them stood inside one of the inner rings, and then they spoke to the crowd.

"Follow us. We are chosen people! Let everyone be as such. Let every person be equal without discrimination! Come! Save humanity and save yourselves!"

Various people shouted from the crowd in response. "Show us the way, chosen ones! Go! If you want to be slaves for the aliens, just go ahead! How do you know who they are, and why they are here? How can you believe so easily? We don't see any danger, other than these aliens that are already here!"

"Ask the scientists, the astrologists!" said one of the men dressed in black.

"Scientists and astrologists? They won't say anything!" someone yelled back from the crowd.

"They do indeed see the great threat!" shouted another man from inside the circle. "The news is true. The aliens are telling the truth, and they're here to help. And even if we do become their slaves, I'd rather live as a slave to the aliens than die in agony here on Earth!"

"This planet is our home!" cried out someone else from the masses.

The argument was broken up by the sound of a blast from above. With a sudden swiftness, a glowing blue egg-shaped object swooped down onto the people inside the circle. It quickly scooped them up and disappeared again, but as soon as it vanished, four of the men were spotted again—falling fast and slamming hard to the ground inside the circle. After that, the circle threw them behind the crowd. The incident completely startled everyone.

"It's a circle of death!" someone screamed. "Let's get out of here!"

Panic broke out, with people stomping on one another in their rush to get away—as far away from the circle as possible.

"Todd, please do something!" Adrian pleaded as he watched the scene below from the ship.

"There's nothing I can do. Everyone must pass the inspection; that's how the program works everywhere. We do not bring criminals with us." Todd then issued another command. "Order all Pitagons and everyone else in the hall! Blend in with the people, and try to persuade them to step into the circle before it's too late!"

"This is definitely going to cause trouble!" said one of the eldest Pitagons.

"We can influence them without being seen. Use invisibility!" Adrian said.

"That ability doesn't always work flawlessly on Earth because of the interference of the gravitational zones. If they notice us, then even fewer people will listen to us," said the Pitagon elder called Todd Pitagon.

Adrian was nearly frantic. "Let's take over every public broadcasting station; let them only hear our voice! Are we going to halt the works of lifting the city?"

"We completed the initial repairs that were necessary to get the project ready," Todd answered. "Now, we just need your power to put the mechanism in motion, but we have to wait for the right moment. I will let you know when the time has come."

Chapter Eighteen

⊱ ⋅ ⊰⋅◉⋅⊱ ⋅ ⊰

New Law

Todd looked pleased with their accomplishments thus far, but he knew there was much more to do. He summoned a Pitagon and gave instructions in a weary but determined voice. "I'd like you to bring Lilla Pitagon and Adrian Pitagon before me. I hope their short rest and the healing force helped them recover and block out all the bad thoughts. I hope only positive ideas are running through their heads now. I don't want their work to be interrupted in the future."

Shortly thereafter, the two old Pitagons appeared in the hall. After everyone greeted them with a bow, Todd stepped forward and said forcefully, "Let my words speak directly to Adrian, Lilla, and their Pitagons! I want you to go among the people of Earth and carry out my last command. Bring before me ten earthly humans who do not know about the impending disaster and who have not heard of the way in which we help people leave the planet. Adrian, I will give you special permission to find your best friend and bring him here to our city. I'm certain that we will need his assistance at some point."

"We will leave immediately," Adrian responded. He walked swiftly toward the door, directing the others to follow him out of the hall.

"Hold on!" Todd said. "There's an unsettled matter still waiting to be resolved."

Adrian turned to look at Todd. "I suppose you mean John and Susanne from the other dimension."

Todd nodded. "Yes, we have to close their case. As we can't be sure if they're dangerous, I have made the following decision. Let's put them on board one of our Eagle mother ships sitting in space near Earth; specifically, the one that will head for the planet Steel, not Kyara. They will end up in another galaxy that will be more suitable for them. I hereby confirm my decision. Put John and Susanne into the transformation chamber!"

Two Pitagons went to the chamber right away, where Susanne and John were waiting for them.

"I thought you'd forgotten about us, my Pitagon friend," John said nervously. "Tell me, little man, who will become our guides?"

"We are your guides," one Pitagon said. "We'll follow you to the end of the world if we must, toward a new galaxy. My name is the same as yours; I'm John Pitagon." He bowed before John.

John and Susanne bowed to their Pitagon guides in return.

John Pitagon then directed the two humans, "Now, step into the conversion chamber. You will become young and beautiful."

"Oh, how long I've been waiting for this moment!" Susanne rejoiced.

"Your transformations will live up to your dreams," John Pitagon assured the pair, "and it will take only a few hours."

The elderly couple entered the chamber and the doors closed behind them.

Back in the Great Hall, Todd continued detailing the next step in the plan for the transportation of earthly humans. "We have to tell people that we'll take all of them, without question," he instructed. "And we won't take anyone's life. Those who are not accepted onto the two Eagle mother ships will be put aboard our smaller Eagle mother ship, and they will take a long journey toward a new planet in a new galaxy. We still need a leader for that smaller ship, and I'm keeping an eye on the chosen humans, John and Susanne, as they will be first to get on board as soon as their conversion is completed. Two of the oldest Pitagons will become their guides, both of whom have provided consistent and valuable assistance. They possess great knowledge and vast abilities. Therefore, hear my new decree!" Everyone sat erect and leaned forward slightly to show Todd they were paying close attention. "Reprogram each ship to accept all humans, according to this new strategy. The order of Solomon, the greatest of kings, must be carried out."

Adrian looked at Todd with a puzzled expression. "This is a substantial change!" he argued. "Are you saying that from now on, we will take the criminals as well?"

"That's what needs to be done in order to give people confidence to step into the circles. People have to know that the circles will not kill them. Otherwise, few will dare to enter the rings, and our mission will fail. We can't use force. Humans must decide their own fate—whether to die on this planet or live on an alien planet with our help."

Those in the hall applauded Todd's decision and bowed to him. Adrian, Lilla, and their Pitagons also faced the members of the assembly, and they slowly bowed in farewell as they headed for the Eagles that would fly them to their new assignment.

At the transformation chamber, the door opened, and John and Susanne stepped out as young and beautiful people. They looked at each other in amazement, and John had tears in his eyes. Their love for each other was completely evident.

"Would you walk the path of happiness with me, Susie?" John asked playfully.

"You are in a very funny mood, John," Susanne responded. "But I feel giddy as well. Perhaps I *will* take the path of happiness with you."

"What a gorgeous lady," John said, beaming.

Susanne slipped her arm through John's and then looked over at the leader. "Please, Todd," she said, "give us great assignments to occupy ourselves. I feel we can do anything together."

"Be on your way to one of our Eagle mother ships out in space," Todd directed them. "You will command that ship, which will accept every human who is not transformed—these will be the people who were not deemed suitable during the inspections; those who were considered bad. They will live a short life, as is normal for them, but it will be filled with hardships in return for their becoming undeserving survivors. Their exile to another galaxy is not a punishment but an act of mercy. They will forget their families and will have new ones. Their gift is life itself, which they can live out while it lasts. We will be able to follow how well these earthly humans are capable of reestablishing their existence in that particular place." Todd waved his hand at John and Susanne dismissively. "Get aboard our third spaceship, along with your guides, and may good fortunes be at your side at all times."

John and Susanne bowed as they backed out of the hall. "Thank you for your trust," John said in parting. "We are happy to serve on this mission. And perhaps our lives will not be as short as the lives of those we will lead."

Todd raised his hand and motioned to the couple to wait. "One more thing …" he began. "Now I can safely declare that you two have indeed become chosen, so you will be able to live for several thousand years. You are not able to reproduce, but you will live life on your own terms, as leaders of a new land in a new galaxy."

Susanne rushed forward, extending her hands toward Todd.

"Thank you for the long life, the youth, and the health, faith and trust."

Todd quickly stepped back from her as he saw the force flare up from the woman's hands and then recede amid yellow and red bursts. "I see your power is at your fingertips," he said. "You truly are a chosen one. Be cautious with your energy, Susanne. Learn to handle it well; otherwise, you might harm your fellow humans."

Then John stepped forward, also extending his hand to Todd in farewell. This time, Todd didn't step back, but he didn't offer his own hand either. They stood firmly facing each other, and both of their minds projected the same thought—that John did not receive power or great knowledge, only youth and renewed health. At that moment, it became clear through the revelation of power that the true leader of the third ship was actually Susanne.

Todd then turned back to Susanne and said, "You have been given the honor as a woman, a member of the weaker gender, of possessing this mighty power, and now you are the leader of the third ship and its entire crew and population. Always be just, as you will decide the fate of many whose lives could be in your hands. Your mistakes will be reflected in your power throughout your life—the greater the error you commit, the more power you will lose. If you should make too many mistakes, you will one day completely run out of power. Always let your decisions be fair and measured."

John stood close to Susanne, and his eyes were smiling as he listened to Todd's pronouncement of Susanne's power and authority. The two chosen Pitagons stood behind John and Susanne, and together, the four of them bowed to Todd and then to all the others gathered in the hall. They walked to the area where their travel spheres awaited, though only the outline of the spheres was visible to the eye. As soon as they stood inside the outlined circle, the travel spheres started glowing with blue and yellow light. Each sphere enclosed a body and then flew up to the sky in a matter of seconds. Those in the hall applauded the event, even as they looked questioningly at Todd.

Chapter Nineteen

>⊷⊶⊙⊷⊶<

A Mysterious Mission

The assembly gathered in the Great Hall witnessed a new event that was projected from within Todd's eyes. They watched as Adrian and Lilla arrived in the city of Miami inside a travel sphere. It was a dark night, and the yellow and blue glow of their travel spheres brightly shined, lighting up the backyard in which they landed. As they slowly descended, the outlines of Adrian and Lilla appeared to partially eclipse the bright lights, and then their images came vividly to life. They exited the spheres and walked carefully and silently toward a house. The outline of the rings from their spheres remained faintly glowing behind them—this was an indication that the spheres were standing by and ready for takeoff at any moment. This backyard was dotted with various kinds of vegetation— flowers and trees—all of which were gracefully arranged on the spacious lawn. The shadows of two human figures could be seen in the dark behind one of the trees. Within a few moments, the shadows moved—the two people were walking toward the glowing rings.

"Look, Borzas, they are back!" one of them said. "I knew they'd come here. This is our chance to swipe their awesome ride. Let's get in quickly and disappear!"

Each person stepped into a ring, each of which only showed an outline of a faint glow of a circle. At that moment, the two men happened to notice the two Pitagon guides standing nearby. Borzas stepped out of the circle and shouted to his friend, "I can't believe they're here again! They always get in my way! I can't go with you now. I have unfinished business here."

His friend looked around wildly. "Borzas! What are you doing old buddy?" he called, unsure of what he should do. "Come back here! This is our chance!"

"Get out of the circle!" yelled Borzas. "These midgets could mess this up for us, and we would get into major trouble."

"Come on, Borzas! We'll just get out of here, and that's it!"

Borzas shook his head determinedly. "This was a mistake. You don't even know where to go!"

"Up into the sky," his friend said breezily, "to follow the path of the stars. And if you won't come with me, I'll just go alone."

Before either men could say another word, they heard the strong command of Adrian Pitagon. "Step out of that circle!"

"And what if I won't?" the man called out.

"You might burn up and turn into dust as soon as the ring

fires the ignition of the travel sphere," Adrian Pitagon said calmly. "Now step out immediately."

The man hesitated for only a moment before jumping out of the ring. As he did, the travel sphere lit up brightly and glowed with a blazing red light.

"You stepped out just in time," said Lilla Pitagon.

Borzas stepped closer to the Pitagons and said defiantly, "What are you two doing here anyway?"

"We are doing our duty, carrying out orders."

"What orders?" Borzas chuckled.

"We are to take you with us to transform you into productive men—men who can serve our highest king," Adrian Pitagon answered.

"You're lying!" Borzas snapped. "There are no kings in the world anymore!"

"There are kings in our world," Lilla Pitagon said. "Three of them, in fact, and we have only one God above all."

Lilla and Adrian reappeared in the yard, along with Adrian's best friend. Astonishment was written all over the young man's face, and he couldn't take his eyes off his transformed childhood friend.

"Let me introduce you to my best friend!" Adrian said as they approached the two Pitagons.

Lilla Pitagon stepped forward, offering a handshake to Adrian's friend. "Welcome!" she said warmly. Streams of yellow light sparkled out of the Pitagon's hand, and the sparkles landed on the young man's hand. Then a purple light beam twisted around him until it fully embraced him. Adrian's friend was startled and didn't know what he should do. "Uh … Adrian?" he said questioningly. The light lifted him up in the air, and then gently put him back down onto the ground. "Wh-what was that?" he cried out in a frightened voice.

Adrian patted his friend on the back reassuringly. "Nothing to be afraid of. It was just a test to determine if you are fit to come with us or if we have to leave you here."

"What is the result, if I may ask?" he inquired nervously.

"You may join us!" Adrian said, the smile on his face growing wider. "You have been chosen! Step into the circle!"

The boy stepped into the circle, and the travel sphere whisked him away.

"Where did he go?" Borzas wondered out loud.

"He went to our biggest Eagle mother ship in space," Adrian Pitagon answered. "He will work under the direction of Jupiter in the future."

"Will I see him again?" asked Adrian.

"Yes, you will soon work with him. But first, we must do as we promised to these two individuals standing before us."

Adrian studied the two men. "Will they also come with us to the underwater city?"

"Yes, we'll take them to the city," replied Lilla Pitagon. She pointed to the men and said, "You two stand in the biggest circle, right next to me!"

Borzas drew back. "Why?" he asked.

"Stand in the circle," she repeated. "We are going to the conversion chamber and then on about our business."

The two men stood upright, and the Pitagons fixed their eyes on them as they reached out with both of their hands. Blazing red beams of light rushed from their palms and wrapped around the two men.

"What are you going to do with us?" asked Borzas.

"We'll teach you obedience," Lilla Pitagon answered, "so that you will not think evil thoughts. So go on now to be transformed!"

The light beam kept wrapping around the two men and placed them into the large ring, which immediately turned into a travel sphere bound for the underwater city.

The men soon arrived in the city and stood before Todd, who paid little attention to the two new arrivals. Todd's eyes closed, and when he opened them again, he no longer saw the images of Adrian's little group. Following that, he called for the attention of the people assembled in the Great Hall.

"The time has come to lift our city so it may serve as the final refuge for much of mankind," he announced. "We absolutely must save the unspoiled natural human race in order to save our own kind. The operation will proceed under the direct control of two chosen scientists from Earth who grew up together and have been good friends since their childhood. Their names are Frank and Joe, and they have been collaborating and assisting each other throughout their professional careers."

Frank Sr. and Joe stepped forward in their converted forms, standing tall and looking young. They greeted Todd and members of the entire assembly by taking a respectful bow. Then Joe began to address the gathering on positive note.

"On behalf of my friend Frank and me, I would like to thank all of you—our ancestors—for coming to us and transforming our lives by the process of rejuvenation. It's a great feeling to be young and strong again. We thank you most of all for granting us the opportunity of a super-long life. We are honored to have the privilege of someday telling the story of how our ancestors helped us reach the age of 950 years. I'd also like to thank my friend Frank for thinking about me when he needed assistance organizing a strange voyage. What he thought was impossible on that day has become very much possible today. Initially, we set off on a journey to find my friend's grandson who was lost, but along the way, two great miracles happened to us. Things like these are truly unbelievable for earthly humans such as we are, and it's a dream come true to have the chance to live such a wonderful reality."

After Joe's speech, Todd walked up to the two scientists to give each of them a heartfelt embrace. His joyful expression was proof of his satisfaction with their work. Stepping away from Frank and Joe, he turned to make another announcement to everyone in the hall. "According to the orders of our greatest king, Solomon, four million Pitagons will soon arrive on Earth from aboard our third largest spaceship. These Pitagons will be deployed all around the world with only one mission: to save humans. We must rescue as many people as possible from the planet, and we have a very limited amount of time. There is no way to know exactly when the asteroids will collide with Earth, but we have estimated possible time frames."

Todd was silent for a moment, and then his eyes began to project another picture. This time, the assembled people saw the image of Pitagons boarding the largest spaceship, along with countless Pitagons briskly boarding hundreds upon hundreds of smaller spacecraft, all of which were launching toward Earth.

I believe in love and in a joyful world,
And a smile at the wind that flies like a bird.
I love to live, and I love to love,
Helping to heal and giving enough.
I look for kindness, and I find grace,
Grasping the miracle of life in this beautiful place.

—Elizabeth Palas